"The characters in Jared Yates Sexton's stories are desperate. They are obsessed. They speak a language that is part barfight, part howl, part brokenhearted country song playing on a skipping vinyl loop. These are stories you want to listen to as much as read, full of fierce and searing and melancholy truths."

—Chad Simpson, author of *Tell Everyone I Said Hi*

"The stories in Jared Yates Sexton's *An End to All Things* are, indeed, about ends—of relationships, of dreams, of innocence—but they also speak eloquently to the means of these ends. Laced through with booze and betrayal, and populated by half-witted quickwits and good eggs with bad karma, Sexton's stories get under your skin, split your ribs, and worm their way heartward."

—Tom Noyes, author of *Spooky Action at a Distance*

an end to all things

an end to all things

Jared Yates Sexton

An Atticus Trade Paperback Original

ATTICUS
BOOKS

Atticus Books LLC
http://atticusbooksonline.com

.

ISBN-13: 978-0-9840405-1-3
Library of Congress Control Number: 2012946578

Typeset in Baskerville by David McNamara / sunnyoutside
Cover design by Jamie Keenan

ACKNOWLEDGMENTS

Some stories have previously appeared in the following publications: "Just Listen" in *BULL*, "Old" in *The Emerson Review*, "What're We Talking About Here?" in *The Raleigh Review*, "A Man Gets Tired" in *PANK*, "I Know I Am Deathless" in *The Benefactor*, "They Put a Shovel in Your Hand and You Dig" in *Inkspill*, "It is Wide and It is Deep" in *Prime Mincer*, "You Never Ask About My Dreams" on *AtticusBooksOnline.com*, "He Maketh Fire Come Down" in *Hobart*, "The Right Men for the Job" in *10,000 Tons of Black Ink*, "Everybody Must Give Something Back for Something They Get" in *Platte Valley Review*, "Loose Him and Let Him Go" in *Relief*, and "Now I Am Become Death, Destroyer of Worlds" in *Pulp Modern*.

CONTENTS

This Book Is For

PAM
NRB
JWS
JRS

JUST LISTEN

Please. For once. Just sit down. No, I'm not telling you to shut up. Just listen to me, okay? Sit down and listen because I've got something I need to say.

Hob and me were working down at that shop, the one next to the Shell station, and we pretty much had the place done, everything taped and primed and edged out and we're just waiting to roll it. But first we took lunch out on the stoop, and we're out there eating peanut butter crackers when one of the women who works there—the one Hob is always going on and on about—she walks over to us with a couple of sacks in her hand. Turns out, she bought us some sandwiches from the deli down the street. And that just about beat all, you know? This woman, the one Hob's so in love with no less, taking time out of her day to go and grab us some sandwiches. It really just blew us away.

No, that's not all. Why would I sit you down to tell you about some woman bringing Hob and me sandwiches? Why would I get all in a huff over that? This is just what I mean—you can't sit still for just a second and let me tell you something. All right then.

So we've got these sandwiches. I've got turkey and Hob's got ham. And they're on these real chewy rolls and all dressed up like the really expensive ones. And we're eating them and Hob's talking about how he's gonna tell that woman how he feels about her, that these sandwiches just beat all and he's going to march right in there and ask her to marry him. And I couldn't help but laugh. You know how Hob is always saying things without meaning to follow through. And I was telling him so, saying there's no way he was gonna do that, and then Hob turned to me and said, You know what I haven't had in a real long time? You know what I haven't had in months? A nice, cold, bottle of coke.

I started thinking and I knew that's what the day called for. This day was so good and different, with the sandwiches and all, and what would really hit the spot right then was some coke. So I told Hob he was right, we should get us a bottle or two and celebrate these sandwiches. He jumps up and before I knew it we were marching next door to the gas station.

We get in there and the place is all kinds of busy. Like all of downtown's in there on their lunch break. It was about noon and you know how it gets. And here we are with all these people, Hob and me in our overalls all splattered white and we must smell like a can of KILZ 'cause everyone was giving us looks. But me and Hob don't care, we got those fancy sandwiches in us and we're about to buy cokes. It's just too good a day to have a care in the world.

Anyway, there's this cooler in the back where they keep all the drinks. You know how they are. But this one's bigger than any I've ever seen before. Rows and rows of every drink you could ever imagine. All these new kinds of cokes I've never heard of. Diet ones and orange ones and fruity ones, you name it they've got it. Once we find the regular cokes we pick out a couple and get ready to head to the counter, but Hob says he wants a candy bar too. I say fine, just pick one out so we can finish up and get back to work. And I'm standing there listening to him rattle off all these candy bars—Milky Ways, Snickers, Crunch bars, all that nonsense—when the bell above the front door goes off and I look up to see this woman walking in. And I don't mean to upset you or get you all mad now, but she had to be the most beautiful woman I've ever laid my eyes on.

I know you don't want to hear that, but let me finish. Let me finish and you'll see where I'm getting at. You don't have to like it, but you need to listen. If you ever do one thing I ask you to in your whole goddamn life, just listen to me right now.

This woman, she's wearing a black skirt and a jacket that goes with it. And she walks over to the coffee bar, where everyone gets their coffees ready, and she pulls a cup out and fills it up from one of those machines. The whole time Hob is next to me, reading off candy names like a little boy. But I'm not listening to him. Not really. I'm watching this woman fill up her coffee cup.

What you have to understand is that she was so careful with it. She made sure to stop before it got too high in her cup, before it got too full to put in her stuff. She set it down on the counter and picked out a creamer tub, and when she opened it she pulled the foil back as slowly, as carefully, as anyone I'd ever seen. Then she got a packet of sugar and tore the corner and poured it in the coffee too. She stirred it in and brought the cup up and took a big, long smell, like she was checking to make sure it was just right, you know? I'd never seen anyone be so careful with a coffee before. Not even close.

Something about the way she was handling that coffee really struck me. I guess you could say it just spoke to me. Something about the way she stirred it and took care of it, like it was a baby or something, that just did it for me. I thought to myself, this here is a woman who gets it. This here is a woman who knows what she wants, who's got her priorities in line. And I'm going to tell you something. You're not going to like it, but I'm going to tell you anyway. What I said earlier about that woman being the prettiest woman I'd ever seen? I knew right then I was going to have to go up and tell her I thought so.

Now sit back down. Come on. Think about someone else, for a change. Think about all the times I've let you go on and on and on and been fine with it. I'm almost done, so just sit there for two more seconds and let me finish what I have to say.

So, anyway, when that woman had finished with her coffee and took it up to the counter I grabbed Hob and told him to pick out his damn candy bar so we could go up there too. We got in line behind her and that woman smelled just as good as she looked. Something about the way she smelled reminded me of how the air gets after a storm. Calm, you know? Just about the most perfect smell on the face of the earth, that's for sure. And a part of me wanted to reach up there and tap her on the shoulder, and tell her exactly what I told you I wanted to say. Say to her, excuse me, I don't know you, but you need to know you're just about the most beautiful person I've ever laid eyes on. Just like that. Not trying to get her into bed or anything, not at all. I wasn't looking to bed her. I just needed her to know. It was real important, right at that time, to let this person know just how goddamn beautiful I thought she was.

But I didn't. I couldn't do anything. I didn't have it in me. She paid and walked right out the door. I was feeling about sick enough to die, honestly. Sick enough to die. And goofy-ass Hob jumps up to the register and starts paying for the candy and the cokes, and I was just standing there, sad as all hell, watching that woman walk to her car.

Now, what I'm going to tell you, you need to really listen to. Because I'm not going to repeat it. Just this one time—that's it.

Okay.

I was watching this woman walk out to her car, this woman holding the cup of coffee she'd been so careful with, the same woman I'd thought was the most beautiful person I'd ever laid my eyes on, when it happened. I didn't even hear a noise. I don't think there was any noise. Her head exploded. Just like that. It burst like a balloon. And the rest of her, that black jacket and skirt, her legs, shoes, all of her, just slumped down onto the ground. That was it. There wasn't anything else. Just her on the ground and all that blood. Coffee spilled all over the parking lot.

I couldn't say anything. Hob started yelling—Oh my God, and all that. He was losing it bad and knocked one of our coke bottles off and it busted on the floor. The guy behind the counter picked up the phone and called the police. Said we might have a sniper or something. Said it like he'd been saying it his whole life. We might have a sniper. Like he'd trained for it. Like it was just another day.

I don't get it. I really don't. The only thing I know is we've got to talk about this—you and me and how we can't seem to get along. All this fighting and screaming and throwing shit.

We've got to get down to the meat of it. All the lying and finger-pointing and the hate. We've got to get down and really talk about these things. I mean it. Some things around here are gonna have to change.

OLD

I feel old. Never did before, even when I was getting up there in years or when my hair started turning gray. I was too busy working the line at the cord factory. But they laid me off and now I sit out front of my sister's place, watching the birds and feeling old.

It's not so bad really, wasting the day away with a beer in your hand. We live near the airport, so every few minutes a jet goes flying by. At four my sister pulls in the driveway and out jumps her and my snot-nosed nephew. While she goes in to make dinner, he sits down next to me and crashes his toy cars together in the grass.

Never been married, but that's not a problem. I met the love of my life in a night class at the high school. It was for folks who made it their whole lives never learning to read. Sarah read textbooks and said it made her feel better to be around all the illiterates. After we made love, I'd listen to her talk for hours. She'd go on about her family and her ex-husband, but mostly about how much she loved reading physics textbooks. She said they were all about how everything works, how gravity is just the earth pulling at us. How everything that leaves must return. The other day a buddy of mine from the plant told me she's shacked up with Gary Richards, my old foreman. I've found you can't believe every bullshit thing someone tells you.

═══════

My sister, bless her heart, has never been a cook. Her spaghetti's mush and her potatoes are nearly raw. I sit at the table and drink from a cup covered in cartoon ladybugs while the boy kicks his feet and slurps his food. My sister asks how the search for a job goes and I tell her fine. I can't stop thinking about starlings. They're mean bastards, gathering in the trees and crowding out the bluebirds and the robins. I keep a twenty-two by my lawn chair to scare 'em off. I like lining them up in my sights. Sometimes I take the shot.

I clean my plate out of respect, then head downstairs to my cot in the basement. It reeks of mold and I can't help but think of the break room where Sarah and me took our lunches after I got her hired. We'd sit and talk about nothing at all while the maintenance boys came and got cokes out of the machine. Some days she'd wait until it was quiet and undo her blouse and flash me her breasts. It was the kind of love you wouldn't know anything about.

═══════

Same buddy called last night and told me Gary and her were taking off for the Tropics. Factory threw them a party and

everything. Big crystal punchbowl and grass skirts. The whole
nine yards. I say that's fine, she can do whatever she wants.
She's a grown woman after all.

Honest, I worshipped the girl. When she got on nights—
when she started working with Gary—I got off my shift and
cleaned for her. Dusted the tables and vacuumed the floor. Beat
our rugs on the rails of the porch. Got on my knees in the tub
and scrubbed the walls. In the morning I'd catch some sleep
on the couch while breakfast cooked on the stove. I ran myself
ragged and all I got was a kiss on the cheek. She was growing
away from me.

It's easy to lay the blame on Gary, that fat bastard. He's the
type who's never worked a day in his life. Soft hands and just
enough bullshit on his face you can hardly stand it. His office
was always open 'til a pretty girl got in there. He told us stories
in the bathroom. To think about Sarah and him at the beach is
enough to kill a man. In a year I never saw her in a bathing suit.
Some things just aren't fair.

I've still got my birds though, hopping from branch to
branch. I see the blue ones wash one another, their beaks picking through their feathers. They take off and fly as if they're
leaving and sit right back down. Sometimes I think of Sarah
like that, like maybe she's just stretching her wings. Maybe she's
circling and looking for a place to land. Maybe I am her perch.

Then my birds dash away as a plane comes growling
through. Big fucker flying over, its belly shining, heading due
south. I can see in the window, can see Sarah sitting next to
Gary. She's holding a drink in one hand and his pecker in the
other. She's saying wait 'til no one's looking so she can unbut-
ton her blouse. I pop a round in my twenty-two and I'm leading

the nose of that plane. I'm cradling the butt against my shoulder and squeezing the trigger. I'm watching that big metal bird
tumble toward the horizon, trailing smoke the whole way. I'm
remembering the rule she taught me so well. Everything's gotta
come down.

WHAT'RE WE TALKING ABOUT HERE?

You got to understand.

Understand what? he said.

It was back when Daddy visited, she said. Back last May.

He thought of her father. A sailor from South Carolina with a patchy beard and gray eyes. He'd visited the spring before. Threw his things in the corner and wasted no time pouring himself a drink. Made himself right at home.

You were drinking so much, she said. Drinking almost all the time.

For a second he looked at the glass in his hand. A ring of foam was all that was left of his beer.

I slowed down, he said. Ain't got drunk near as much lately.

I know, she said. Thank God you slowed it down. I didn't know what was goin' to happen one day to the next.

So what was it? he said. What was it you wanted to tell me about?

11

She said, Well, I don't know. I mean, I do, but I don't know how to say it.

Just say it, he said. Just belly up to the bar and say it already. Goddamn.

It wasn't me, she said. It was Daddy. He brought it up. That night he took us to eat at the oyster bar.

He barely remembered that night. He barely remembered any night from that period. He'd ordered one drink after another on the old man's tab. And when he woke up the next morning, the weight of the world resting on his skull, he stumbled into the living room and found that Daddy and his bags were gone.

You got to understand, she said. You were like an animal. Nobody knew what to do with you.

He got up and poured himself another drink. That a fact? he said.

You yelled about God knows what, she said. Yelled and sang and when Daddy asked you to quiet down you put your hands around my neck and squeezed.

Huh, he said, and sat back down.

She said, I mean it. You were scary back then.

He took a draw from his beer and leaned back in the chair. He said, So he said maybe you should split, huh?

No, she said.

I bet, he said. I bet he told you you'd find someone else who'd put up with all your bullshit and be fine with it.

No, she said. Daddy didn't say that.

I'll be goddamned, he said. I'll be goddamned.

We got you home, she said, and you tore down all the pictures in the bedroom. When I came to bed you were on the floor, crying about someone named Josephine.

Did Daddy say you could move back to South Carolina? That you could move home and get away from your big, bad husband?

I wish you'd get it, she said. You were like an animal. She lit a cigarette and tapped her fingers on the table. An animal, she said.

When he finished his beer he got up and washed his glass out in the sink.

He said he knew someone, she said. He said all it would take was a couple thousand. Everything would be taken care of.

He put his glass down and faced her. She had the cigarette in her hand. It was burning down to her knuckles. She was looking out the window at something.

He said this guy was good, she said. That he knew him from a ways back and the guy had a reputation.

Slowly, he sat down. He reached for her and touched her leg. What's that? he said. What're we talking about here?

Daddy said I could just let him know a day, she said. And that I should go to the store or go for a drive. It wouldn't take more than an hour he said.

Wait, he said.

I still remember, she said. I still remember what Daddy said. Sharon, he said, that man is a good-for-nothing sonuvabitch and he's gonna wind up killing you someday.

He tried to make her face him, he put his fingers on her chin and cheek, but she didn't budge.

And I said okay, she said. I said as soon as possible. Call up your friend. Get the wheels moving.

They sat there, the two of them.

Sharon, he said. Sharon.

He was going to use a bat, she said. He was going to kick in the door and beat your head in with a baseball bat.

He sat there in his seat, watching her look out the window. Finally she looked down at the cigarette and ashed it in an ashtray on the table.

I went to the store, she said, just like I was supposed to. You were on the couch. Passed out. I kissed you and you woke up to tell me to pick up some chips.

Sharon, he said.

She said, I drove to that store, thinking about what I'd see when I got home. Your body on the floor. Blood on the walls. Bits of brain and hair and bone.

He looked at her looking out the window again. Something darted past, just a shadow of something, but he looked out himself and tried to see if he could make out what it was.

I called Daddy, she said, and told him to call it off. Told him I thought maybe there was some good to you. Maybe you'd sober up and make a real go at being a man.

He listened, but he was still watching. Something was out there. He could feel it. Felt it so much it made his gut sick.

What'd he say? he said.

She looked at her cigarette. She studied it. He said I hope so, she said. That's all he said.

They sat there some more, the two of them at the table. Before too long she stumped her cigarette out in the ashtray and told him she was going to bed. He said okay, he'd be there in a few, but he didn't move. He sat right there, in his chair, his eyes trained out the window, at the big yard behind their house. He was waiting for that something to move again. He thought if maybe it moved again he could get a good look and figure out what the hell it was. Figure out just what he was dealing with.

A MAN
GETS TIRED

When Sally drank Sally got ugly. Didn't matter where we were. Could've been at the White House for all she cared. She'd get a couple shooters in her and start speaking up. Talking shit to anyone who'd listen. Got me in a few scrapes along the way, that's for sure. Seemed like every Friday I had to finish a fight Sally started.

Most of the time it was good old boys. Bunch of young fellas hard as chain-link fence. Drinking straight with a beer kicker at the bar. She'd see them standing there, bullshitting, and she'd walk up like she was bulletproof and tell the biggest one of the group he was a pussy.

Got to the point where I was used to it. I'd be sitting there trying to down a pitcher and I'd feel someone walking over with purpose. It wasn't so bad if there was one or two, but they liked to travel in packs. You'd be laying into a guy and feel some hands on the back of your neck. Then you'd get worked over. Some nights I'd drag Sally home and put ice on my busted face while she passed out on the bed.

Once, I said to her, please, can you lay off? She didn't understand. Sober she was as sweet as a saint. I don't know what to do, she said. I said, Hey, you're gonna kill me. That's what I said. You're gonna kill me if you keep this up.

For a while she was better. I'd get home from work on a Friday afternoon and the two of us would make a nice dinner and drink a little on the porch. Watch the neighbor kids walk around. We'd talk and things got back to normal. I was healing up and getting used to the peace and quiet.

Then she went out for drinks one night and called me close to three in the morning. Said there was trouble. I drove down and by the time I walked in there was this guy with a shaved head grabbing her by her shirt. Didn't even have the chance to take off my jacket before she had me in it.

It got so bad I told her I couldn't do it anymore. I said I loved her and wanted the house and babies and everything we'd talked about, but I was afraid I was gonna end up dead one of these days. It's like Russian roulette, I said. Every time I look up there's someone gunning for me. A man gets tired, I told her.

I know, she said. Whatever you want, baby.

So I stayed. We went back to the dinner and drinks routine. We'd eat and talk and make love. There was a point there where I had everything I ever wanted. A nice life to come home to, a good woman there to take my hat. Then the friends called and asked where the hell we'd gone. They were asking what'd happened to us and why we never went out anymore. They were drunk on the message. It was Thursday.

The next day Sally dotted on her makeup and fussed with outfits for an hour. She kept saying how much she'd been looking forward to it, getting out again. She said she was so happy just to get a night out of the house she could scream.

Harper's was busy by the time we got there. That was our bar. On Fridays they put out a spread. Everything you could imagine. They had specials on the beer and they played music that'd set the world on fire. It was beautiful and I almost forgot all of the trouble Sally'd put me through. She was being kind and the two of us kept sneaking off to the dark parts of the bar and carrying on like a couple of kids. Beautiful. That's what it was.

I didn't think there could be a better time. I mean, we were all having a decent go at it. Sally and me and our friends were keeping to ourselves and minding our business. Then they walked in.

There wasn't a doubt in my mind they'd be trouble. He was one of those fellas who wore cutoff shirts and tight jeans so he could show off the body he'd earned in the weight room. His hair buzzed just so, to piss you off. He was looking for a fight. And on his arm was his girl. An over-tanned broad with the biggest fake tits you've ever seen.

I mean, they were massive. You could feel everyone in the place looking at them. Nobody even bothered hiding it. And the thing is, that sonuvabitch seemed to eat it up. He pulled down the top she was wearing and gave everybody a peek. A half-hour in and he was taking money from fellas for pictures.

Sally didn't see at first. She was too busy downing her sweet and sours. That was fine by me. I knew if she looked up and saw those two that'd be all she wrote. And then she did.

What in the fuck is that? she said. She put down her drink and wiped her nose with her palm. Just who the fuck do they think they are?

I said maybe it was time to leave. Maybe we'd had enough.

No, Sally said. No, no, no. What in the fuck is that?

My buddy and me bought another round and tried to get her attention off it. That couple was at the bar. The woman had her top lifted up and the fella was telling guys to do a shot off her. Real crazy shit.

I'll be fucked, Sally said. She had already gone through another sweet and sour and she was starting on a new one. I'm gonna goddamn say something.

I tried to talk her down. I said, Honey, just have a seat and we'll have some drinks and a good time. But at that point, she was up. A boy with red hair was resting his head on one of that woman's giant breasts. The man was holding a camera and taking a picture.

Hey, Sally said to them. You should know I think this is bullshit.

What's that, baby doll? the man said. What'd you say?

She said this is bullshit, the woman said with a laugh. She thinks this is bullshit.

Well, the man said. He slammed the camera down on the bar and it shattered. Fuck you, he said.

I was up there by then. Fuck you, I said. Fuck you and your goddamn doll, I said.

The man didn't even bother squaring off. He pounced. One second he was standing there and the next he was on top of me. I've never seen anyone move so fast. We rolled on the floor and knocked against some chairs and tables. He was working his knee into me and butting with his head. Everywhere I turned he was hitting me.

Next thing I knew I was being held back from the bastard. I don't remember the whole thing too good. Just a lot of elbows and teeth. The hard wood in my back. I put a hand to my swelling jaw and me and Sally ran out as the bartender screamed that the cops had been called and everyone had better get out. We listened. We packed up and left fast as we could.

I was quiet the whole way home. Sally was doing enough talking for the two of us. She was going on about the man and the woman and how disgusting she thought the whole thing was. She couldn't believe how some people treated their women. She couldn't believe how some women let themselves be treated. I was busy looking at all the dark houses along the way. I was thinking about all the people safe and sound asleep, happy as could be.

After we got home I helped her into the bedroom and got her clothes off her. I stripped down her jeans and had her lift her arms so I could slide her shirt off. She turned in the covers a few times 'til she was wrapped up nice and tight. She was talking as I went to the bathroom to check myself out.

It just defies explanation, she said. It defies explanation that people live like that.

I was looking at myself in the mirror. The man's fist had dug trenches into my forehead and cheek. The bruises were growing and some blood was leaking out of a cut below my eye.

Some people, Sally said.

She got quiet. I put some spray on my hands. They were cut up and my left one felt like it was broken all the way through. No matter how I moved I hurt.

Hey, Sally said when I slipped in beside her. Hey, honey. Next week let's stay in. Is that okay?

I tried to get comfortable and pulled the covers over my aching body.

Maybe we'll make some dinner, she said. Fry up some bacon and do breakfast. Beat some eggs and fix some toast. I'll make the coffee, she said. What do you want? she said. What do you want, honey?

I KNOW
I AM DEATHLESS

I was sitting in my kitchen and enjoying a nice, hot cup of Millstone brand instant coffee the day my neighbor Harry came by and told me about the problem he was having. It was a little after eight and the woman I'd slept with the night before had just hurried off to work. She'd gone in such a huff that she'd left her designer Louis Vuitton handbag on the counter next to my Whirlpool stove and range.

So, there I sat, wondering if I should go through her designer Louis Vuitton handbag right then, or wait for a better, more appropriate time later, when there was a knock on my door. Standing there, looking as down in the dumps as I've ever seen him, was my neighbor Harry.

Why so sad? I said. What's the matter? Would you like a cup of Millstone brand instant coffee?

Sure, Harry said, taking a seat at the table across from mine. I'd like that.

I made a cup and handed it to Harry. I noticed, as he took

it from me, that his hand was covered in charcoal smudges. See, Harry was a painter, an artist, and I figured he must have been working that morning.

Tell me something, I said, watching Harry take his first sip. Do you prefer Millstone brand instant coffee or Folgers brand?

Harry's sad face lit up. No question about it, he said. Millstone brand is the best. It has the fuller body taste to it. It goes down smoother.

I couldn't agree with you more, I said. Did you know more restaurants serve Millstone brand instant coffee than Folgers brand anymore?

I didn't, he said. No, I didn't know that.

It's true. Now, tell me why you're so sad, Harry.

He took a long drink from his cup. I was sketching a woman from down the street today, he said. She's still in my apartment right now, waiting.

Was this a nude sketch? I asked him.

Harry did all kinds of paintings, some of pieces of fruit or sad, lonely-looking people, but the ones I liked best were the pictures he painted of naked women standing or lying around.

Yes, he said. She was nude and on my bed. And this girl, you might have seen her before—she's pale and works at the GAP department store on Wailings Street—

I know her, I said. I'd seen her many times from when I'd gone in to buy a new GAP cable-knit sweater or GAP favorite-tee undershirt. She had short red hair and perfect, grapefruit-shaped breasts that strained the fabric of her black GAP turtleneck.

So, he went on, I'm sitting in a chair, trying to sketch her and her perfect body but I can't. The TV in the corner is turned on and on the screen is an episode of the television show 'Live with Regis and Kelly.'

Regis Philbin and Kelly Ripa, I said.

Yes, he said. And they're talking to someone who's just won tickets to something. Maybe it was the Super Bowl. Maybe it was the World Series. And I've got this wonderful creature on my bed, the most beautiful woman I have ever seen, and I cannot take my eyes off the television.

Huh, I said.

I'm just watching them talk to this person, he said. This fat man with thick glasses and greasy hair, and I can't bring myself to turn away.

I took another sip of my Millstone brand instant coffee and thought about my neighbor, my friend, and his problem. I tried to imagine sitting in his bedroom and looking at that wonderful girl from the GAP department store. I pictured her stretched out across the sheets, her hands lost in the curls of her short red hair, her white body glistening in the morning light with her thighs parted a few precious inches. I imagined not being able to look at her, not being able to pay that beautiful girl any attention, and nearly wept. Harry's sadness made me so sad I had to find something to cheer him up. That's when I saw the designer Louis Vuitton handbag sitting on my counter next to my Whirlpool stove and range.

Listen, I said to Harry. The woman I slept with last night left her designer Louis Vuitton handbag behind. Would it make you feel better if we went through it together?

Harry nodded and looked as if he might start weeping out of appreciation. When I got up and grabbed the designer Louis Vuitton handbag off the counter, I noticed it was lighter than

I'd expected. I set it on the table Harry and me were sharing and opened it slowly and carefully, the way a surgeon might do. To our surprise it was filled with dozens and dozens of packets of Sweet'N Low artificial sweetener. We took turns reaching in and pulling out fistfuls of the Sweet'N Low artificial sweetener packets. By the time we were finished we'd found there was nothing but Sweet'N Low artificial sweetener packets in her designer Louis Vuitton handbag.

Harry, I said. Let me ask you something. Which do you prefer: Sweet'N Low artificial sweetener or Splenda brand artificial sweetener?"

Harry looked down at his smudge-covered hands and frowned. He said, I like Splenda brand artificial sweetener very much, but I can't say I've ever had Sweet'N Low artificial sweetener.

I thought it over and went to my cupboards. I sorted through my boxes of Lipton Iced Tea beverage mixes, my cans of Hormel brand Hot N Spicy Firehouse Chili, my canisters of Morton's salt and Hershey's cocoa, and found the canary yellow plastic tray I'd bought at a Pier 1 Imports store to hold my packets of Splenda brand artificial sweetener. I put them on the table and picked a couple of mugs I'd purchased at the same Pier 1 Imports store and filled them with more of my Millstone brand instant coffee.

Listen, I said. I'm going to sweeten one cup of Millstone brand instant coffee with Splenda brand artificial sweetener and another with a packet of Sweet'N Low artificial sweetener and we'll see which you like best.

Harry seemed thrilled with the idea and even closed his eyes while I sweetened the cups of coffee. To make the test even

harder I switched the cups around a few times. When I'd finished I asked Harry to open his eyes and take a drink.

This is very good, Harry said, taking a drink from the first
cup. This tastes like I'd expect a cup of Splenda brand artificial
sweetener sweetened cup of coffee would taste. Pale and yellow,
almost, broad strokes of blue.

He put the first cup down and took a long, careful draw
from the second.

This has to be the Sweet'N Low artificial sweetener. Brings
to mind pink fields with musical notes drifting through the air.
I like it. I really do.

Harry finished what was left in the cup and I could see, as
he set it down, that his frown had vanished entirely. What was
left was the happy-go-lucky Harry I knew and loved best. He
kept nodding, as if to say thank you, my neighbor, my friend,
for sharing with me these wonderful cups of Millstone brand
instant coffee and for opening my eyes to the wonderful world
of Sweet'N Low artificial sweetener.

Say, he said, still grinning. Was I right? Was that the order?

I nearly agreed to be agreeable, but when I looked down
at the mugs I'd bought from the Pier 1 Imports store, the same
one where I'd purchased my canary yellow tray, I saw they were
identical with no discernible differences, and I realized, in the
excitement of the moment, I'd forgotten to make note of which
cup was which. Unable to hide my uncertainty, I looked up and
met Harry's worried eyes with my own.

We looked around my cozy kitchen in my cozy apartment,
from my Whirlpool brand range and stove to my Whirlpool
brand three-door refrigerator with ice maker and water dis-
penser. We looked at the boxes of Lipton Iced Tea beverage

mixes to my cans of Hormel Hot N Spicy Firehouse Chili, to my canisters of Morton's salt and Hershey's cocoa. We looked to the packets of Splenda brand artificial sweeteners and the packets of Sweet'N Low artificial sweeteners. We looked and we looked and we looked.

THEY PUT A SHOVEL IN YOUR HAND AND YOU DIG

You don't ask questions. You don't complain. You get in line and you get in the truck. When you get out and you're standing in front of a big hole, you don't ask how. You just dig and you dig with every goddamn thing you have. You dig until they tell you not to dig anymore.

The heat doesn't bother you after a few days. Day in, day out. Bending over, chucking dirt. Ain't got time to bitch about the heat. No time to bitch about water. You got to get your arms in rhythm. Ticking like a clock. Don't pay any attention to the dirt in your teeth. The sweat on your lip. The whole world's just a patch of dust and rock right in front of you. Nothing more, nothing less.

Seems like every minute you're about ready to fall over. About ready to just drop. Fall down to your knees and just get a second more to breathe. And that's all it'd take. Just that one second. That's all it'd take to make the day right. But they're right behind you. With shotguns. Ain't afraid to use them either.

You take that second and you got a load of shot in your shoulders. A whole world of nothing good.

Then you get back on the truck. Just when you think you're ready to stick that shovel right in your heart they tell you it's time. Sun's going down. Time to get home. Get cleaned up. Tomorrow's another day.

Don't expect much to eat. Maybe some bread. Maybe a cup of water. Some days neither. Ain't no use complaining. They'll give you food when they want to give you food. That's what you learn the most. They give you the food when they want to give you the food.

After a while you get used to the hunger. The way it rolls around in you. You get to the point where you talk to it. Get to know it a little better. And there's different kinds of hungry. Don't let anybody tell you different. There's hungry on a cold day and there's hungry in the summer. Anybody tells you different, they haven't been hungry before.

And there's nothing to do, really. Just sit on the ground and look at the splinters in your hands. Used to have cards but they took them away. Took everything. Books. Pencils. Everything.

Sure, there's a TV. Right there in the hall. Sits on the news all day. Boys in suits and ties. Arguing about whatever. Typing on their computers. Sometimes music plays and The President comes on. Says this is good and this is good. War's going pretty good, all things considering. Lots of boys dying, every day. Families crying over lives gone too soon. You learn to tune it out. You learn to look straight ahead at the person starving across from you.

I'll tell you this. Couple years ago there was a boy working the line. Twenty maybe. Real put together. Came in asking questions, just like you. Said he wasn't going to settle down. Was gonna make a fuss every chance he got. First night he smarted off to one of the guards and got a club to the face. Those boys in black don't play around. They get you down on the floor and they work you over a bit. Make sure there ain't gonna be trouble no more. And they had that boy bleeding. Bad.

Around then we were working this big hole outside of Oklahoma City. Biggest goddamn hole I'd ever seen. Looked like the world grew a mouth and would've liked to have swallowed us down. Took ladders just to get to the bottom. Every day we climbed in that hole and dug some more. Must've been two hundred of us. Digging and digging. Who knows what we were digging for. Who knows if we were digging for anything.

Then one day the boss came out and said it was time to fill the hole back up. That we needed to climb out and start filling it. Everybody looked around. We'd already lost a dozen or so men. We were red from the sun and everyone was just a minute or two from keeling over.

So we climbed back up. That's all we could do. We climbed back up and most of us got to work filling that hole. Not that boy. That boy hadn't learned his lesson, I guess. Those guards working him over didn't get the message across. He had something to say. He had something he really needed to say.

He dropped his shovel and walked right up to the boss who'd given the order. He put his dirty hands on him and gave him a shove. He said there wasn't no way he was going to fill that goddamn hole. He said there wasn't no reason to dig it in the first place and there wasn't no reason to fill it back up. He said he'd rather die than pick up another shovelful of dirt.

And do you know what they did? They shot him right in the fucking head. They tossed him into the hole. They got on their bullhorns and told us to get back to work. And do you know what we did? We got back to work.

You'll learn before too long. You'll get the idea. They put a shovel in your hand and you dig. That's what you do.

IT IS WIDE
AND IT IS DEEP

The night before the raid I dream of Virginia. The sky is the soft blue and purple of my boyhood and I'm standing on the porch, back on Dad's farm, looking out into the woods. There're shots and a rushing, someone out there running dogs, maybe treeing a coon or two. I know it's winter, but it's my dream and I'm able to make it just fine. I heat the air as easily as reaching for a thermostat and the whole world's a little warmer.

There's nothing but trees and shapes, but I know these woods like the rooms of my house and I take turn after turn, brush past the branches, and move through. I keep reaching out toward the heart of it, the clearing in the middle where I know I'm heading. I've lived this moment a thousand times if I've lived it once.

When I get there I see Davey Hutchins, a short and angry man who walks with a terrible limp. The right side of his face is frozen in palsy and the corners of his lips sag toward his chin. He has a rifle, but it's tucked beneath his arm. One of his dogs, a bloodhound, squats at the base of a tree and points upward. Davey's squinting and trying to make something out.

It's a girl, he says. There's some kind of girl up there a howlin' and carryin' on.

A girl? I say.

Yep, Davey says. I'll be goddamned if there ain't some kind of girl up there.

I go and take a look for myself. It's dark, but looking up into the cradle of the branches, and against the light of a fat moon overhead, I'm able to see her soft curves. She's braced against one of the limbs with her head thrown back.

Davey scratches his chin and yells. You a girl? There a girl up in that tree? He sounds confused at first but his voice gets an edge to it. He's shouting now. Come on down, he yells. Come on down or I'm gonna start shooting.

When she comes down it's easy to see she ain't got a stitch on her. Just as naked and free as anything you've ever seen. Long brown hair filled with knots and briars. Dried spit and dirt caked on her face. Big heavy breasts. She has a seat on the ground. Davey drops his rifle and mumbles something I don't catch. That bloodhound hides behind his legs. The girl reaches up and paws at her cheek.

If this ain't the best day of my life, Davey says, I don't know what was. Came out here looking for some coon or squirrel and got me a wife. Goddamn if this ain't the best day ever.

Before I can say anything he's lurching toward her and just about ready to have his way. The girl looks up at him and you can tell she's not real happy. She grimaces a little, bites her lip. Davey's already getting down in the grass with her, reaching to undo his belt and unzip his jeans. Before he gets down on his knees I pick up his gun and put the barrel to the back of his head and give him a little nudge.

Best be getting off that one, I say. Best just let her be.

You cocksucker, Davey says, not even turning around to face me. I don't know what you think you're doing, Harry, but you shouldn't be doing it.

I look past him and see the girl. She's all kinds of confused.

Turn around, I tell Davey. Turn right around here.

He does and I'm looking into that messed up mug of his. I trace the sad curve of his mouth with the barrel. He's so fired up he's starting to shake.

I say, If you don't want your pecker shot off you better zip up.

In no time he's reaching down and putting himself away. He turns and I use the barrel to nudge him back to attention.

Now what you're going to do, I say, is get up and walk away from here. Got that?

Fuck you, he says.

No, I say, fuck you. Fuck you and get up and walk away. I'm not asking.

Davey doesn't move an inch.

Last time I say it, I say. Get up and leave and you never saw shit. Got it?

This time he doesn't even wait for me to finish. He takes off into the blackness of the wood, that bluetick trailing the whole way. I hear him limping through the brush and then nothing. I'm left with the girl.

I take off my coat and drape it around her. Already she's cooing and squirming to get in my arms. I take her and hold her close. I kiss her and it tastes like fresh-tilled earth. She's pulling me atop. Leaning back and spreading herself across the coat and the ground. I lower myself down onto her and thrust. I know she is my one and only.

———

The mess is mostly cleaned up before we get there. A cloud of smoke hangs heavy in the air and there are a dozen or so bodies burning in the sun, but the shots are in the distance now. Taped to the dashboard of the Humvee is a picture of my one and only wearing a checkered top and sprawled across a blanket.

I get out and take me a look around. There's a row or two of captures over by the wall of a grocery store and they're lying on their stomachs with hoods over their heads. Some of their legs are kicking and their bodies flopping around. They look like catfish snapped ashore. A group of bored men stand watching from a distance, their hands in their pockets.

Eleven in all, my assistant says. Three more in the building. Got a team coming in to unload munitions.

How many we lose? I say.

Two, he says.

I say huh and wander over to the rows. There's a kid lying there, fifteen maybe, his hands bound behind his back and his hooded head thumping against the sidewalk. There's a wet stain dripping from inside his pants down to his knee. I put the point of my boot into his ribs and give a little shove. I say, Got a pissin' problem?

Our boys are huddled over by the caravan. They're taking a knee and got their weapons on the ground. They're tired and worn and one of them is holding his left hand with his right. Blood gushing down his wrist.

I'm so taken by the sight I start to tear up. If there's one thing I hate to see it's a soldier with a busted hand. Dad came home from Okinawa missing three fingers and never got over it. Sometimes I'd see him sitting there in his chair, looking over his mangled fist. It just about broke my heart to see anyone suffer like he did.

My assistant calls my name and steals me out of my memory. He starts talking and points to one of the men lying face-down in the road. All I hear are the words High Level and Priority.

———

In the basement, in a hallway past the bathrooms and the janitor's closet, is a room. In the room is a table and a sink. When I come in the fucker's already strapped down by his ankles and wrists. There's a belt around his shoulders. Always a hood. Haven't ever seen a face and never care to.

There are two guards on either side and I tell them to fill the buckets. I straddle him and the table like I do my darling wife and, leaning down, I say, This had to happen. There are so few of you and so many of us. I am sorry you are weak.

A signal and the first of the buckets hits his face.

That is an ocean, I say.

Another comes down and his fingers claw at the table. His feet click together and there's a groan. Some words, but when I look at the translator he shrugs.

Do you know what ocean that is? Do you know what ocean you are drowning in?

Nothing but cries.

That's the American Ocean, son.

The translator tells me he has phone numbers. Addresses in Manchester.

And the American Ocean is wide.

A ledger in Pakistan. Notebooks with bank accounts.

And the American Ocean is deep.

A gurgle.

I say, The President's a good friend to have. He tells the water when to rise and when to fall.

Through his hood I stroke his face. Water seeps out of the cloth and I dip my fingers into its pools. I say, The President is a friend of mine. In the summer we clear brush and share iced teas on his porch while the massive sun sets over the Texan hills. You can hear the cattle bay in the evening breeze. He is a very good friend to have.

There is only howling now.

━━━━

The doctor holds up cards smeared with ink. It bunches and forms arcs and splotches that look like things. Don't worry, he says. I mean, I understand I don't know quite what you've gone through over there. Not having been and all. We're here for you and as soon as we get this over with we can get those checks coming right along. Good? Good.

The first looks like a car and I tell him so.

And this? he says.

A house with a chimney, I say.

This?

A plate of steak and eggs.

He nods and shuffles the deck. One more, he says. One more and we can just talk for a bit. Get this whole thing over with. How about this?

There are ripples, as if someone had dropped a pebble into a sea of ink. They radiate out and toward the corners of the white card while the rock sinks.

There are ripples, I say. As if a pebble was dropped into a sea of ink.

Good, he says. He signs something and nods again. Very good.

———

My boys spring out of the house and rush down the drive to meet my car. I've barely stepped out before they tackle me and shower me with kisses. Their hair is parted perfectly and they wear tailored tweed jackets. They are beautiful and they are my blood.

On the porch is my wife, wearing a yellow summer dress that barely contains her heaving chest. Her hair is loose and fanning over her shoulders.

You were missed every night and every day, she says.

I sweep her into my arms and press my lips against hers until neither of us still has breath. From there it is to the bedroom where she strips off my uniform in the proper order of jacket, tie, button down, slacks, and socks. She rubs fine oils over my back and chest and tells me when she is of the proper warmth and wetness.

———

A week in and I miss the feeling. I wait at the windows for caravans to come down the drive. While I walk the grounds I listen for fire. I tell my wife and children to prepare for a hunt. We will leave at twenty-one hundred hours.

In the dark we walk into the woods with our rifles. The dogs jet ahead while we trudge down through the ditches and the valley. The moon is high and full and once my eyes adjust I can see everything.

We wind through the trees and take a few shots at some squirrels, but end up empty handed. My youngest, Robert, swears the one he sighted was hit square and has to be bleeding out. So we follow him for a moment, his weapon slung across his back. At seven he is already blossoming into a man. He speaks his mind openly and does not tolerate foolishness.

A little ways south and the bluetick finds it ducked under a sticker bush. The animal is prone and dying. I try and tell Robert to be wary, but he gets down and crawls right in. Lee, my oldest son, follows his younger brother into the brush and they pull the squirrel into the open. My heart beats and swells until it fills my chest. I pull my one and only tight and press my face into her nest of hair. When I inhale I can taste her perfume and it smells of lilac and spring mornings.

Look at these children, I say.

They turn and smile as if they'd heard my words. They prod the squirrel's trembling body with their guns and coo. Lee plucks hairs from its curled tail while Robert runs one young finger across its head, past the eyes and to its mouth. He pulls the jaw and when he lets go it snaps back. It looks as if the animal is talking to us, chattering on about whatever, and we all lean forward, cupping our ears to listen.

YOU NEVER ASK
ABOUT MY DREAMS

At that point things had been rough for a couple of months and I would've done anything to ease the tension. I set an alarm for half an hour earlier than usual. I thought if I had some breakfast going when Cathy got up she'd have to see that I cared.

After all, cooking wasn't the easiest thing to do in our house. Both of us hated doing dishes so the kitchen was always a mess. There were pots and pans stacked on the counters and plates in the sink. Some still had clumps of food stuck to them. I even had to rinse out a bowl to use. Somehow there were a couple of clean forks and knives in the drawer. I got some eggs from the fridge and went to work scrambling the yolks.

While I was tossing in some vanilla and cinnamon I heard this noise on the window. It was this *chit-chit-chit* sound. Real fast-like. It was freezing rain. By the looks of the street that ran out front of the house it'd been going awhile. The stoplight was shining off a layer of ice. A car drove by real slow before locking up and fishtailing. It spun almost halfway around before the driver got it corrected and went on his way.

From the other room I heard Cathy's alarm go off. She groaned and shuffled into the shower. That week hadn't been good to her. We were both finishing up school, her studying and me teaching, but she was in the thick of it and the stress had really started wearing on her.

The thing about Cathy and me was that whenever one of us got to feeling pressure, things started falling apart. The worse it got the more we picked at each other. An argument here, an argument there, until eventually we'd just have a knock-down drag-out and stop talking for a couple of days.

I remember this one time when the both of us had had some kind of trouble at work and the bills were piling up. We got to making smart comments and butting heads. It built up and built up and something ridiculous sent us over the edge. Something to do with me changing channels on the television and she was up and cussing me out and telling me she had a good mind to cut me.

Cut me? I said. What the hell're you talking about?

She got right in my face and started chewing on her bottom lip. It was what she did when she got real upset. James, she said. I've had enough of your shit. You hear me?

There was a look on her face I'd never seen before.

All right, I said. All right.

She said, I mean it. I've never meant anything more in my life.

I know, I said.

Okay, she said. All right.

That night I couldn't sleep for anything. I just kept tossing and turning. All I could think about was what she'd said.

Hey, I said, shaking her awake. Hey, hon.

What? I'm sleeping.

Hey, I said. You know earlier?

What about it? she said.

What you said about wanting to cut me?

Yeah.

You meant that? You really meant that?

Cathy took a deep breath and messed with her pillow. Yeah, she said. I did. If I'd had something to do it, she said, I would've.

That woke me up. Not just that night either. I mean, it really stayed with me. How could it not? Anytime we fought after that, if it got heated or whatever, I'd think about what she'd said and start apologizing real fast, saying I'm sorry and trying to hold her close. You can't deal with that, after all. You can't be looking over your shoulder and sleeping with an eye open every night.

So that's what we were up against, all that stuff piling up and the two of us nearing something awful and permanent. And there I was, dipping some slices of bread in the egg and putting them in a pan on the burner. French toast was her favorite and I was hoping she'd see I was trying and maybe we'd get things back on track.

Cathy walked into the kitchen, dressed in a sweater and jeans and drying her hair with a towel.

Making breakfast? she said.

Trying, I said, and grabbed a spatula to turn the toast. It was getting some good coloring on it.

Today's gonna be a rough one, she said.

I said I bet and turned on the coffeemaker.

Is it snowing out? she said, straining to look out the window behind me.

Freezing rain. Looks real slick.

That's just what I need, she said. I mean, I really want to go and flunk this class and break my arm on the way out.

I laughed and checked the toast. It was just about done so I sprinkled some more cinnamon on top and turned the burner down.

I had awful dreams last night, she said. She had that towel in her hands. She was squeezing it and balling it up before she let go and it fell to the floor. I mean, they were terrible, she said

Huh, I said. I got the toast out of the pan onto one of the few clean plates. From the cabinet I grabbed a bottle of syrup and carried all of it over to the table and laid it out for her.

Did you hear me? she said. Did you hear what I said or do you not care about my dreams?

I said What? and poured a couple cups of coffee.

You never ask about my dreams, she said. I don't think you give a damn what I dream about.

Sure I do, I said. I handed her a cup and a fork and a knife. Eat, I said. Eat and tell me about these dreams.

You don't want to hear about 'em. It's fine. It's no big deal. You don't have to worry about what I'm dreaming.

I said Honey and smiled. I want you to eat and tell me everything you dreamed about last night.

You don't have to say that, she said. I know you're being nice and it's appreciated. I really appreciate it. You need to know that.

I mean it, I said.

All right, she said. She sliced into the toast and dragged it through a puddle of syrup. You don't have to listen if you don't want to, she said. She took a bite and smiled. This is real good. Really good.

All right, I said. Now, what about this dream?

Well, she said. It was one of those where it feels like real life. Like you're really there and you don't know any better. You ever have those?

Sometimes, I said. The freezing rain was starting to really come down outside.

Anyway, it was one of those. It was so real to me. I can't get over that, how real it was. I could smell it and feel it. Everything.

Okay, I said. I was listening but still watching the sleet. It'd picked up to the point where you could hardly see anything for it.

Cathy said, Are you listening?

Sure, I said. I was looking at the sleet. That's all. Please, keep talking.

Cathy sighed and took another bite of her toast. So I was in my old high school and I knew there was this test I had to take, but I couldn't remember where the room was. For the life of me I couldn't remember.

I said, Wow.

Yeah, exactly. You said it. You really said it. And I went to get a schedule out of my locker, but I didn't know the combination.

What'd you do? I said.

I went from door to door but I never found the room. I got so upset I started crying. I could feel the tears rolling down my face. I could really feel them, she said.

I finished my coffee and rinsed it out. Then I scrubbed the pan I'd used. Is that it? I said.

No, she said. That's not it. That's not even close to *it*. If that was it I would've said that was it. I got all the way home and none of the lights would work. I kept flipping the switch but it didn't matter. I was in the dark and it was the scariest thing ever. It didn't feel like home. It didn't feel *safe*.

I said, Huh.

Then, all of a sudden, they all came on. Every light in the house. And do you know what I saw?

What's that? I said. What'd you see?

She set her fork down on the plate. Her eyes narrowed the way they do whenever I've done something to really piss her off. You, she said. I saw you sitting in your chair. You were there the whole time.

I didn't know what to say so I kept scrubbing.

I asked you why you didn't help me and you didn't say anything. Nothing.

When I finished with the pan I turned around to say something, but I couldn't. Cathy was sitting there at the table with her plate of half-eaten toast in front of her. She looked like she was about to cry, just like she did in that dream, but what really got me, what really got my attention, was the knife in her hand. She was gripping it for all she was worth. Gripping it so hard her knuckles went white.

Why would you do that? she said. Why would you just sit there and not say anything?

I thought about it a second. I mean, I really stood there awhile and wondered why I might've done something like that. I thought about it and looked at that knife in her hand. I said I didn't know.

Cathy didn't really say anything after that. She put her knife and fork and dish in the sink with my cup and the pan and all the other dishes and went into the other room to get her shoes and coat. I watched her tie her laces and button her buttons. She stole one last look in a mirror on the wall and went outside to get the car ready.

I stood at the sink and washed our dishes. When I got done with those I started in on the ones that'd been there awhile. From where I was standing I could see Cathy scraping and beating ice off the car. It was so thick she had to hit it with the butt of the scraper. Her hair kept falling down in her face and then she'd have to stop, take a breath, and tuck it back behind her ears, only to have it fall all over again. It took her a while to clean the windshield, but she got through. When she finished she got in and backed down the drive.

It was about time to take off when I was done with the dishes, so I got my coat and gloves and shut off all the lights. The sun hadn't started coming up yet and it was so dark in there I could hardly see to get to the door. I tripped over the couch and a pile of clothes. Outside I breathed the cold into my lungs. I had about a half a mile walk to the school and needed to get used to it. I stepped out onto the drive and tried to find my footing on the ice. It was everywhere, on the houses, the power lines, the street signs. A layer of it coated everything. It was even on the trees, and when the wind blew through them the limbs and branches groaned. They groaned and cried until they were just about ready to break.

HE MAKETH
FIRE COME DOWN

He was on the TV again. That pudgy-faced man strutting up and down the stage. Preaching about the downfall of the species. Working himself up again until he got down on the balls of his knees and cried like a baby. We were watching him, my husband Nick and me.

Goddamn it, Nick said. Goddamn why does he have to be on every time I turn on the TV?

I said I didn't know. Maybe it was because some people liked him somewhere out there. Some kind of sad, hopeless people that slept with their guns and put knives in their doors.

That man was really having at it that day. He was stepping high into the air and proclaiming the evils of the liberals, the follies of the progressives, saying even Lenin and Marx had to answer to God someday.

Fuck, Nick said. Fuck you.

Who? I said. Fuck who?

Fuck him, he said. Fuck them.

═══════

He was on a display at the bookstore. Nick and I went there to look through the back issues of National Geographic. I liked to imagine myself a giraffe tripping through the brush and Nick said he could be a hippo, bobbing there in the dark.

Christ, Nick said, nearly knocking over that cardboard cutout. On it that man was holding a book in his hands and a sign that offered ten percent off the new hardcover edition. Fucking marketing trash, Nick said. Fucking trash.

I said, These are the types of books that end up in old women's yard sales. Scattered among the closeout bins.

Another sign sticking out of the stack of new books said that man was going to be at a signing later that week. Said you could even bring in your merchandise and get that signed. Your door mats and magazines. Any and all of his twelve previously published volumes.

Nick spat on it and shuffled along.

═══════

He was signing books that day and Nick woke me up early and said we had to go. Said he'd never forgive himself if he missed the chance to see the freaks and geeks. Just throw something on, he said, and we'll go down there and get a load of their signs and revolutionary war outfits. For the love of Christ, just throw something on, he said.

So I pulled on a shirt and we went to get breakfast in a little diner across the street so we could watch them line up.

Each one of these people votes, Nick said. I mean, fuck, they get out and vote.

I was watching this woman across the diner. She was looking at how pretty she was in a mirror on the wall.

I'm gonna go over there, Nick said. I'm gonna go the fuck over there and give them a piece of my mind.

I was watching the woman in front of the mirror, so I said okay. You do that.

———

That man was on the TV and across the street at the same time. I sat in that diner and watched him pray for retribution for the socialists and wondered just how somebody could do that. I had a lot of time to wonder because Nick was giving that group of idiots a piece of his mind. Didn't really figure I needed to check in on him.

When we left it was still barely light and I could tell right off something wasn't right. He was quiet. When I turned the radio up because a good song came on he reached for the dial. I asked him what was the matter but he wouldn't turn away from the window.

We got inside. I hung my bag on the hook by the door. I said, Honey, what's wrong?

We need to talk, he said, grabbing a chair from the table. I've been doing some thinking.

You have? I said.

I have, he said. I believe in the wonder and majesty of George Washington and the simple poetry of the Constitution. There is no greater concern than the spread of infant ideas by infant minds. Mine and ours are destinies linked by the same great road many great men have travelled. There is no one God but the one God.

I asked what he was talking about and he said it was time that we stopped fornicating in such a varied way. Any good wife of God's, he said, would submit herself only in the true and proper fashion, that of submission. And then he told me he had a burning heart that beat with the words of Christ and Madison.

———

He was on TV again, preaching to us the value of productivity. John and Abigail Adams went to bed by a quarter 'til nine and so would we. We needed the energy to stand up to the lies and smears of The President and his gang of biased news networks. No one could speak ill of that man on the television and get away with it.

Nick turned off the lamps by the bed and put the TV on the channel that man's always on. By the count of his voice we made love and delivered unto him a new generation of founding fathers. The segment was over by the half-hour and it was on to learning our history and our future.

After that man was off the television and we shut it down, I stayed awake while Nick drifted into an easy sleep. My mind was racing about what that man had said. I had heard him say we held the new tomorrow in our hands. I wanted to ask Nick what he thought that meant. I wanted to ask him about all of the changes, about how everything was turning into something else. How quick it all was. I reached for him, reached to turn him toward me, and my hand caught him there in his chest.

My fingers stayed even though they burned. There it was. That curious, curious heat.

THE RIGHT MEN
FOR THE JOB

It dawned on us that maybe our luck had run out. First the car started coughing and jumping to the right, then the hot water heater leaked so bad it fell through the laundry-room floor. We were trying to lift it out when the kids came running to tell us there was a man in the driveway. He'd hit a cat—our cat—and he wanted to apologize.

Before that everything seemed to be going our way. I was writing for the newspaper and sometimes people recognized me from the picture that ran next to my stories. Mary, my wife, had regular work as a substitute teacher and we were starting to pay off our debts. Our boys Sam and Spencer were happy and growing and never went without. They had toys and clothes and we bought a new car and appliances and every little thing that crossed our minds.

A couple of years passed and everything changed. The paper folded and Mary couldn't get anymore teaching gigs. Something about an argument she'd had with this bitter old woman who taught junior year English. Then our things started breaking down all at once. Every day it was something new. A blender on the fritz. Bad brakes. A broken knob on the TV. Then Spencer tossed a rock through a basement window. Sometimes Mary and me would lie in bed and just list all the problems we had.

One night she asked me what it was that we did wrong.

What's that? I said.

Did we do something wrong? she asked again, flipping her pillow over and punching it. All these things that're happening. Did we do something to deserve it? Something to deserve our lives going all to hell?

I didn't know what to say. I guess at that point I didn't think we were that bad off. 'Course I was drinking a lot and was pretty out of it most of the time. I probably wasn't the best judge.

Mary rolled over so that her back faced me. She sighed. I just feel like it's too much, she said.

I asked her what she meant. I didn't know what she was saying.

I don't know, she said. I'm just talking, I guess.

I reached across the bed and put my hand on her shoulder. Oh, it can't be that bad, I said.

There was a noise from somewhere in the house. It sounded like one of the boys had woke up and was playing in the other room. It really is, Mary said. It really is that bad.

That was a couple of days before the power went out. We were in the kitchen getting breakfast ready when it happened. Mary was pouring the boys' cereal into bowls and I was putting together an old fashioned. It was summer, the hottest pocket of July, and I didn't feel too bad about trying to stay cool.

Mary was saying something about my drinking, something about how I didn't have to start so early, when there was a loud pop. Everything in the house was going before that. TV, air, fridge, a radio by the stove. And then they just stopped. There was a second or two of the quietest quiet you've ever heard, when the boys came in just a-crying about their show shutting off.

What was that? Mary said, turning to me. Just what the hell was that?

I got up and took a look around. The fuses were okay and nothing seemed out of place. The stoplight in front of our house was working just fine. Then I looked out the back window and saw a couple of lines hanging down and into the grass. They were jumping around like a pair of snakes, sparks shooting from their ends.

What is it now? Mary said. She was pacing around the kitchen while I looked through the phonebook for the electric company. Oh God, she said, when's it gonna end?

It was probably a limb or something, I said. Maybe the wind picked up.

The boys were galloping around singing, The power's off, the power's off, clapping their hands and yelling as loud as they could. I called the number in the book and told them there were live wires out there and that they'd better get a crew over in a hurry. We got kids around here, I said into the phone.

Oh God, Mary said. What if somebody wanders over here and gets hurt? Do something, she said. Fast.

I told her I didn't have the first clue what to do and hung up the phone. After that I got everybody into the living room and tried to calm them down. I told them this kind of thing happened all the time and there wasn't anything to get upset about.

The boys handled everything pretty all right. They were asking questions about where electricity came from and what was going to happen next. I told them the work crew would be over in just a couple of minutes and we sat and waited while Mary walked to and from the back window, chewing off every nail she had.

A half an hour passed and I called the electric company again. They told me it wouldn't be but another ten or so minutes until a truck pulled up. Then forty minutes went by. Another call and another ten minutes. An hour. Another hour.

It was hot by then. The heat had been climbing for the past week and was hitting a hundred degrees. The news had told us the night before that some people in town had already died. I believed it. Just being in the house right then, without the air or anything, it was getting pretty uncomfortable. We were all sitting around fanning ourselves with magazines and changing into shorts and loose T-shirts. Mary had to tie her hair back and even then she was sweating. After a while we went into the kitchen and took turns opening the fridge and putting our faces into what was left of the cold air.

You have to do something, Mary said, pointing to the boys and the dark bands of sweat seeping through their clothes. Please, she said.

I didn't have any answers—I mean, what did I know about anything? So I did the only thing I could think of. I made up another old fashioned and had everyone put on their shoes. With drink in hand I led them out the side door that opened to the carport. Just a few feet away was the backyard and those wires. We moved slow and careful and climbed into the car. When I turned the key it coughed to life and sputtered. You could really tell it was on its last legs, but when I messed with the temperature control the air came on just fine.

Are you sure this is safe? Mary said.

I flipped on the radio and found a decent station. The boys were bouncing up and down and singing along to the music. I put my drink on the dashboard and reclined a bit. Sure, I said to her. Nothing's going to get us in here.

That seemed to ease her worries for the moment. She leaned back and closed her eyes, ran her hand across her head and wiped away some sweat. Okay, she said. I mean, what else could happen?

We stayed in that car for a good forty-five minutes or so, just the four of us sitting there and passing time. Some music played and some commercials too. There was even one for brand-new, souped-up air conditioner units, if you can believe it. I laughed pretty hard at that one, but Mary didn't find it so funny. The guy came on and said that if you wanted to experience the cool you deserved, you were gonna have to shell out a few extra dollars for quality. He said nothing comes cheap and then some people talked about how good it felt to sit in a home cooled by so-and-so brand air conditioner. It beats the heat, one woman said.

That's about when the work truck pulled into the driveway. I saw it in the rearview mirror. A couple of fellas stepped out and put on some protective gear. They grabbed poles and tools out of the back of the truck and made their way toward the house. Mary asked me what those things were called and I told her I didn't know, but they looked like just what the doctor ordered.

I got everybody out of the car and we walked back to the side door. As Mary and the boys went in I stayed behind and had a quick word with the guys.

Howdy, I said to them. How you fellas doing today?

Shit, one of them said. He was the older of the two and his meaty forearms were covered in green tattoos. Guessin' we're doin' better than you folks.

I couldn't help but laugh. Here I was, standing there on my carport with a pair of broken lines dancing behind me. Dressed in an undershirt and swimming trunks, no less. That sounds about right, I told him.

The other guy, the younger one, was wearing sunglasses that wrapped around his head. He pulled them off and I could see where he'd been out in the sun so much that the skin under them was whiter than the rest of his reddened body. From his belt he pulled a walkie-talkie and told someone on the other end that they were at the place and to cut the juice. I looked in the backyard and watched those wires collapse into the weeds.

All right, he said. We're gonna fix this up for you in no time.

I took that as my cue to go back inside. Mary had sat down by the back window and looked ready for a show. The boys were already playing like they were electric workers. They had on toy hardhats and carried around their fishing poles like they were those tools the men had. One of them said I'll get your electricity back on lickity-split, but I didn't know whether it was Sam or Spencer. I was too busy watching the men in the backyard.

They walked up to those wires like it wasn't a big deal at all. Just watching them do that put me on edge. I can't stand electricity. Been shocked too many times. When I was younger I helped my dad around the house and had a few run-ins along the way. One time we were fixing up the basement and I got to work on what I thought was a dead outlet. The jolt hit me so hard it liked to have blown my hand clean off. Dad took my tool belt away and said that was that. Watching those guys grab the wires without even a second thought got me feeling antsy as all get out. But I was curious. There was something about the way they went about their work that made it hard not to look on. You could really tell they knew what they were doing.

Look at them, Mary said, not even turning. It's like they're not scared at all.

I know, I said. I went to the freezer and got out a few half-melted ice cubes and refilled my glass. The air wasn't cold in there anymore and I could tell it wasn't going to be long before all our meat started to spoil. Hey, I said to her. We ought to do something about this meat.

Like what? she said. She was still watching the men outside. What're we supposed to do?

I don't know, I said. Take it out? Maybe get some ice?

Sure, she said. Go find some ice. That's fine.

I mean, this could turn into a real mess if we don't take care of it, I said. We've got steaks in here. Hamburger. The works.

She wouldn't turn away from the window. Okay, she said. Get some ice.

After I realized she wasn't going to help, I put down my glass and got the keys to the car. I stepped out there again and stood in the carport for a minute and watched the men some more. The older one, the one with the tattoos, was yanking one of the wires off the house and the younger one had climbed all the way up a pole in the alley. They were working so fast it had to be seen to be believed.

I drove to the grocery store and when I went in the air conditioning felt so good I could hardly stand it. There were a ton of people there, it being Saturday and all, and I walked the aisles without looking for anything in particular. Here were all these people in a hurry with their lists and I was taking my time and really soaking it in. I picked things off the shelves and just read the ingredients. Then I'd put them back down and move on to the next box or can and do it all over again. Everyone was in such a rush that they kept pushing past and saying nasty things under their breath.

Finally I made my way to the back of the store where they kept their ice and booze. I grabbed a bag and then went over to the coolers full of cold beer. That sounded pretty good right then, tossing back a few beers, so I grabbed a case and headed for the register. The line I got into was the express lane and it didn't take no time at all to get to the checkout girl. She was a younger thing, dark hair and light eyes, pretty, with a button on her vest that said Just Be Happy.

I like that, I said, pointing to the button. Just be happy.

Oh, she said, scanning the case of beer and putting it in a basket with my ice. Thanks, she said.

I paid my money and told her to have a good one, but as I walked away she got my attention again. Hey, she said. You're the guy, right? You're the guy from the paper?

Yeah, I said, saluting her with my free hand. That'd be me.

Nice, she said, smiling. She said, Always good to meet a celebrity.

Something about that made me feel pretty good, so I popped open a beer for the ride home. As I got close though, I saw the workers' truck was still there so I went ahead and drove on by and took some back roads for awhile. I cruised the country for a good half hour or so, drinking and singing along to music, happier than I'd been in a real long time. All that driving really did me some good. I mean, the car was behaving for once and the heat wasn't so bad with the windows down and all that cold beer. I even started thinking about that checkout girl and how cute she was. I thought maybe if I went back there, grabbed a thing or two for the line, I could've had a real decent chance at taking her out. Right then, all those things that'd been weighing on me, all the breaking and madness, even Mary's worrying, didn't seem to matter anymore. It would've suited me fine right then to have just kept driving forever.

The sun was going down though and the ice had started melting. I knew I had to get back to the house. The truck hadn't moved, so I pulled around it and into the carport. Before I went inside I looked out into the backyard and saw that the wires had been cinched up and weren't hanging down anymore. Then I heard a humming coming from our air conditioner and knew the power was back on. The men weren't anywhere to be found.

When I got in the house I got my answers. They were set up in my kitchen, around my table, Mary and the boys with them. There were plates full of hamburgers sitting on the table and our ketchup and mustard were out too. The two of them were chowing down.

You get lost? Mary said as I walked in. Forget the way home?

Something like that, I said, putting what was left of the beer in the fridge. Hey fellas, I said to the guys. Thanks a lot. I can't tell you how thankful we are.

No problem, the younger one said. He had a hamburger in one of his dirty hands and he was grinning while he chewed. I tell you what, he said, trying to swallow a bite down. Your lady here can cook a mean hamburger.

You got that right, the one with tattoos said.

Oh, Mary said, laughing. Stop.

I got a beer out and gave the workers a couple. Mary didn't say much to me. She just stood there and asked if she could get them anything or if they were comfortable. Her and me watched the two of them eat in silence for a while. She had a big smile on her face and didn't even hear when the boys asked if they could go into the living room and play some more. I told them yes and leaned against the counter. It was so strange to me, those two men sitting and eating at my table. Watching Mary watch them eat.

Pretty soon I couldn't stand it anymore and went in there with the boys. They had two chairs set up in the living room with a jump rope strung between them. Spencer was using a wrench on it, a real wrench that I figured belonged to one of the men because it was covered in grease, and he was putting its jaws around the rope and turning it round and round. Sam thrummed it like a guitar string. I sat down with my beer and watched them.

Here you go, Spencer said, really having a go with that wrench. Here you go, we're gonna have this fixed up real good.

Sam plucked it one last time and nodded his head. Don't worry, he said. You got the right men for the job.

I watched them like that for a long time. The sun disappeared and it got dark before the workers stopped eating and got their things together. The tattooed one came into the living room and got his wrench back from the boys. Mary was running around asking if they wanted food to go. It wouldn't be any trouble, she said. I could fry some more and wrap them up.

No, the tattooed one said. That's just fine. You're too good to us.

Oh, Mary said. Okay. It was just so nice of you to get the power back on. That really was great of you.

The two of them took turns telling her it was all right and then thanked her for the dinner. She followed them out and I could hear her talking to them on the carport as they walked to their truck and put away all their gear. I was still sitting in the living room, still holding my drink. Sam and Spencer had moved on by then and found another game to play.

When Mary came back in she didn't say anything. She went straight into the kitchen and got the pan off the stove and made up the sink to do some dishes. She scrubbed the grease and droppings off with a pad and rinsed it out under a stream of hot water. She whistled and danced a little while she did it. Everything seemed different about her then. Everything was much lighter. She moved from the sink to the stove to the fridge and cabinets. It was almost like she was dancing.

I saw her from my seat there in the living room. I leaned back and felt the cold air running through. I listened to the hum of all our machines, all our things. I was waiting to see what was going to fall apart next.

I GOT A BIRD THAT
WHISTLES,
I GOT A BIRD THAT
SINGS

The summer after my first teaching gig I needed a change. Something to help blow off some steam. Something to do with myself. So I bought a boat. I found an old one in the classifieds and it was just what I was looking for. From then on I'd get up in the morning and head out to the lake on the other end of town and push off before it got too hot. The rest of the day I floated around with a line in the water and a beer in my hand.

That helped for a while. I got to feeling better about life in general. That is, until one day I didn't. I was floating around that lake in my boat and suddenly I didn't feel so good anymore. I decided to figure out what was causing me so much pain and sadness and after a couple more beers I hit on it.

See, I was married to a girl named Cheryl. She had to be one of the best people who ever walked the face of the earth, but I was tired of her. Tired to the point of losing my mind. Seems to me you have to be so in love with someone you might rip their clothes off any second and I hadn't felt like that about Cheryl in years. She was the mother of my little girl and all, but I didn't feel passionate about her one way or another.

I'm not going to sugarcoat this. I'm not going to sit here and make you think I was a decent guy in strenuous circumstances. I'm not going to bullshit you. I called Marie, a secretary from the department, and asked if she wanted to have a drink. It went from there.

There was something different about her. She wasn't the prettiest girl, not by a long shot. She had this big nose and some pockmarks, but the guys I worked with went nuts over her. She was all they wanted to talk about. Either they were talking about the way she got her hair cut all wild and modern, with streaks of blue or red in there, or they were going on about her corduroy skirts. Whatever it was, they just couldn't get enough.

At first, things couldn't have been better between us. We'd make love all day and talk about the future. She wanted me to leave Cheryl and move out east. Said I could work on my book while she got her master's. It all sounded so good and right at the time, the two of us trudging around Maine or upstate New York and getting a life together. Pretty soon I was losing interest in everything else and finding excuses to get out of the house. I'd start fights with Cheryl and tell her I was going to a hotel. I lost all sense of right and wrong.

It soured though. Marie started drinking and going out with co-workers and I wouldn't hear from her for days at a time. Or, she'd call my house at four or five in the morning and wake the family up and I'd have to lie and say it was a buddy from back home. It got real confusing there for awhile. And sometimes, when she called, I'd hear some guy in the background asking her to come to bed. Asking who was on the phone. I got the feeling she wasn't being faithful.

I started going to the lake again every once in a while. Just like before, I'd push off in the morning and float around all day. I sat there in the sun and drank my beer and thought about how I was doing Cheryl wrong. Really it was just awful what I was doing. She was a good and decent woman. Pretty too. Prettier than Marie, that's for sure. She had this long dark hair and a little upturned nose. And what a wife she was. She cooked the best dinners and brought me and the fellas drinks when we played cards. And she loved me.

She told me once she loved me so much it hurt. Sometimes, she said, I get a pain right here when I think about how much I care. She put her hand over her heart. It gets so bad I have to sit down.

I tried my hand at being a decent husband again. Whenever I got back from the lake I helped around the house and took the laundry down to the basement and watered the lawn. I came up from behind and put my arms around her and told her how much she meant to me. The whole thing put her in such a mood she couldn't stop smiling.

But that didn't last either. I got to thinking of Marie and everything with her seemed better than before. I remembered the good times, lying under the covers and discussing Joyce and Foucault and everything else under the sun. I thought of the nights we'd stay up all hours watching movies and ordering Chinese delivery. I called her and things started up again.

This one morning, after we got back together, I was driving to fish at the lake a little bit when I felt this need to go see her. It felt like I was being pulled to her and I couldn't help but take the turn into town and head over to her place. I parked the truck and boat in the lot and was climbing the stairs when her door swung open and out popped Bill Wolfson, a poet I worked with at the school. His clothes were rumpled and his hair looked like he'd just woke up. He stepped onto the porch, grinning ear to ear, and stretched his arms out real wide and yawned like a character on television. Then he saw me coming.

Charlie, he said. Charlie…how the hell are you?

How goes it, I said.

Stopped by to pick up some papers.

That a fact? I climbed up to the step he was on and got my chest right up against his. Where they at?

Bill looked at his hands and then to me. I wanted to grab a hold of him, but when I got ready to Marie came out onto the porch. She was brushing her hair, the same hair Bill and all the other guys loved so much.

Now, most girls I know would lose it at that point. They'd probably start crying their eyes out and apologizing like crazy. Not Marie. She was the kind of girl who would lie straight to your face and smile. She just kept brushing her hair and looking around like nothing was wrong.

Morning, she said. You know Bill, right?

Bill didn't wait any longer. He slid past me and hustled down to the parking lot. Marie stepped calmly down to where I was and grinned.

Any chance we can give him a ride? He doesn't have a car here.

I was really steaming at that point, so I said Give him a ride yourself.

What're you so mad about? she said, pulling the brush through her hair. We were at the bar and he drank too much. What was I supposed to do? Leave him there? Besides, my car got picked up for the shop this morning.

All in all, I was about to tell her what she could do with her car, her hair, and Bill, when she moved past me and grazed her breasts against my arm and that was that. The three of us got into my truck—Bill, me, and Marie stuck in between. A turn of the key and we were down the road.

There was an awful silence going until Marie flipped on the radio. She sped through the channels and settled on some old rock 'n roll. She even had the nerve to turn it up. I couldn't stop thinking about her and Bill. He was the kind of guy who slept with any student who'd have him. The whole thing seemed so dirty and wrong that going home to Cheryl and the kid didn't seem so bad anymore.

When the station started playing "Knockin' on Heaven's Door" Marie cleared her throat and turned to Bill. You know, she said, I met Dylan last winter.

I knew the story well. She'd been at a bar in Albany with an ex of hers, a real obsessive British Literature professor, when who should walk in the door but Mr. Robert Zimmerman himself. He sat a couple stools down from her table and asked if she had a light. They talked John Wesley Harding for the better part of an hour. Before he left he tossed her a book of matches.

It was a story I'd heard at least a dozen times and I wasn't in the mood, so I shut it out and thought about Cheryl some more. I thought about how maybe I could just set her down and lay it all on the line. I thought maybe I could spill my guts about the whole affair and she'd be hurt, sure, but would come around and forgive me in the end. I always thought she'd break down and I'd hold her until she was ready to talk about it. That we'd probably make love and in the morning things would be back to normal.

We didn't end up having the talk until the fall after that summer. And when I told Cheryl about Marie she didn't say a word. She just got up, went to the bathroom, and threw up. Over and over again. She threw up until there wasn't anything left. Then she got our little girl out of bed, dressed her in her coat and shoes, and carried her to the car. She left. She drove off. She was gone for good.

A few months after the whole ordeal she called me one night. She was drunk and saying crazy things. Olivia's in bed, she said. Olivia was our little girl. I've got some towels stuffed under her door and I've got the oven on, she said. The door's open, Charlie. I could die. I could really die.

I hung up and called the police and they went and picked her up and put her away for a few days. Olivia came and stayed with me for a month while Cheryl dried out. Those were some rough times.

But, before any of that, there in my truck with Marie and Bill, I was thinking about how god-awful of a situation it all was. The heat was a bitch and I was starting to really sweat at that point. And there, right next to me, was my so-called girlfriend and a man I saw in the hallways every morning. I couldn't wait to dump both their asses off and head home to my wife.

I could tell Bill wanted out too. The whole ride over to his place he was fidgeting and sighing and rolling the window up and down. The whole thing was so ridiculous I had to laugh. I got a beer out of the cooler under my seat and offered him one.

Twenty minutes later we pulled into the drive of a duplex on the other end of town. Bill hopped out and ran to his front door. He was moving so fast he didn't even shut the truck door behind him. After Marie reached over and slammed it shut she got out her purse and lit a cigarette. You up for some breakfast? she said. Maybe some coffee?

I didn't say anything. I was letting my pissed off build up until I could finally tell her just what I thought of her.

Are you going to pout over this? she said. C'mon now.

I just backed out into the road.

He didn't have anywhere to go, she said.

I said, He could've called a cab. He could've called a cab from the bar and gotten a ride.

At three in the morning? she said. She blew a long stream of smoke that drifted toward the windshield and curled back. Whatever happened to hospitality? Whatever happened to basic human decency?

This is over, I said. I'm done. I'm not going to be cheated on with someone I work with.

Marie laughed. Cheated on? Need I remind you who you sleep with every night?

It would've suited me just fine, that second, if I never spoke to Marie again. I just watched the road as I drove back to her apartment, and I was almost there when she said, Listen, if you wanna to pout over this whole thing can't you at least do it over eggs?

I wanted to say no, but it made sense. Maybe we could sit down for one last breakfast and go over all the ways we messed up and walk away with clear minds. Besides, the beer had hit my stomach and I was starting to get real hungry, so we turned around and headed downtown. Most of the way there I was thinking of ways I was going to be a better husband. I was going to be home more and do more for Cheryl. This time I was really going to keep it up. Then Marie reached across the seat and put her hand softly on my knee.

I was used to that kind of thing considering every time we ever got into a fight Marie would push and push until I'd realize just how terrible of a person she really was. Then I'd get away from her and leave her apartment or scoot all the way over in the cab of my truck as far as I could. The whole time I'd do that I would just think about how lucky I was to have Cheryl in my life. After a little while, though, Marie would always slink over and get a hand on me. That confused things, made my conclusions foggy all over again.

We went to this little hippie diner for breakfast. It was the kind of place that opened late and closed early. The waitresses all had ratty, unwashed hair and the cooks wore beards. Our waitress had a shaved head and she led us outside to the deck out back where there were some white plastic tables set up with silverware and umbrellas. Behind the deck was a small park full of trees and gazebos. I ordered some coffee and an omelet and Marie had the French toast.

Marie spent a couple of seconds chewing on ice from her water until she got out her cigarettes again and lit up. Out there, on the back porch, all we could hear were the cars going by on the street and the birds in the trees. I sat there looking at her, trying to figure her out. I was always trying to figure her out. It seemed like sometimes she couldn't have been real. She never worried and, even though she wasn't the prettiest girl, she was never without her fair share of men. She broke up two marriages before mine. Something made them keep coming.

I asked her if she was sorry and she took a drag off her cigarette. She brought it out of her mouth and looked at it intently.
She always did that, like she was surprised to be smoking. Sorry
about what? she said.

Sleeping with him, I said.

She smiled and said, in the shittiest of tones, Are you sorry
you slept with the wifey last night?

I didn't want any part of that so I waited for the food a couple of minutes before going inside to wash my hands. There was
a payphone by the bathrooms and when I saw it all I thought
of was Cheryl. I thought maybe I could call her. Maybe I could
reach out through the phone lines and my voice could travel the
miles between us, over the wires and past the poles, and land
right there in the house and find her. Maybe I could start to peel
back the pain.

I reached for some change but couldn't find any. I considered making a collect call, but thought better of it. How could I
explain the noise from the kitchen? People talking and eating in
the background? Marie's voice if she snuck up behind me and
whispered into the receiver?

By the time I got back my food was there and Marie was
pouring some syrup on her toast. I sat down and sliced open my
omelet. Onions and peppers spilled out. We didn't talk. We just
ate. We ate and watched a family playing in the park.

I was almost finished when it happened. A starling, so
black it looked like it'd been dipped in oil, flew out of the park
and landed on the patio a few feet away. It stood there, taking us in. Then another landed right next to him. Took off
and came back again. Wasn't a second or two until a whole
storm of them came and started fussing and biting at each

other. They'd land, fly away, and come back, as if they were tethered by something.

Marie dropped her fork and watched them. Isn't that something? she said.

They came and went. A cloud of them swirling through, their chirps gathering. They scattered and took up on a chair or table or fence and then dove right back into the fray.

Why're they doing that? Marie said.

I said I didn't know. I mean, who knows why birds do what they do?

It went on a little bit longer until they just stopped. Like that. They just quit and flew off and it was just Marie and me and our food. We finished and I got the check. I handed the cashier a twenty and got back a fistful of change. Marie went to the bathroom and left me next to the payphone.

I sat there thinking about the things I could say to Cheryl to make it all right. I could bring up the old days when we were happy just having a couple of drinks and watching some old movies. I could tell her I loved her totally and completely and that none of this running around business ever meant anything in the first place. I could be honest for once. I could belly up to the bar and take what was coming to me. I could tell her how terrible of a husband I'd been and how I was going to do better. That there was a better part of me.

I dug out a quarter and held it for what seemed like a good long time. It wouldn't have been that hard, getting a hold of her. She was home after all. She would've picked up the phone. She would've listened.

YOUNG & EAGER

When Becca said we needed to talk I couldn't help but expect the worst. I'd heard it before after all. Everyone I'd ever loved had said it. They wanted to talk about affairs, about hidden relationships, about lost love and other symptoms of waning affection. It meant revelation and it meant, more often than not, goodbye.

She said, We'll make dinner tonight and talk it over. I was popping some waffles in the toaster when she said that and I couldn't do anything but walk off and get a tie out of the closet. When I came back she was still sitting at the table, nursing a cup of coffee.

Tonight then? I said.

She nodded. Sure, she said. What do you feel like having?

Doesn't matter to me, I said.

Becca cradled the cup with her hands and got this look on her face. I knew that look. She got it whenever she was disappointing someone. I'd thought she was a decent woman inca-

75

pable of doing wrong, but in that look I could see regret clear as day.

With my breakfast finished and the plate in the sink, I grabbed my bag and keys from the hooks by the door. I told her to make whatever she wanted and walked out to get the car.

At work I ground through the day. I kept thinking about all the talks in my past. Marsha, the first and the harshest, had fallen in love with my best friend and said it was my fault. Lauren had wanted women and Terri said, with no emotion, that she'd been confused and had never loved me after all.

Thinking about them made it even harder to picture Becca doing something similar. She was so kind and gentle that I couldn't see her pulling that kind of shit. I'd known this woman and the sort of good she possessed.

I considered every possibility. There was a week she'd gone to Ohio to visit a sick uncle. Maybe she'd met an old flame for coffee and the conversation had led to a nearby Motel 6. Maybe it was an ongoing thing with hushed calls in the middle of the night and letters hidden in some camouflaged shoebox. Or a fling at a gas station or the supermarket. A quick meeting of eyes over a produce display. Rough sex in a closet with shelves of chemicals and paper towels. Nails and teeth in flesh.

It got to be too much. Thinking of my Becca, picturing her in all of these twisted and secret positions, broke my heart and I sobbed like a child. I put my head in my hands and mourned some secret I didn't even have a name for yet.

When I came home I found her spooning cheese into noodles and rolling them in a pan. She ladled some sauce on top and put them in the oven. She was wearing the yellow sundress

I'd bought her for Easter. I went in the bedroom to change out of my clothes and clicked on the TV. After flipping through I settled on a ballgame I couldn't have cared less about. I put on some jeans and flopped down on the bed.

What had me so confused about the whole thing was how sure Becca had always been about us. Even in the beginning, when I had been wary of love, she'd been so patient and reassuring. She told me once, on the way home from a party, that she was beginning to believe in fate. That she didn't believe in some kind of god or cosmic architect, but she had a suspicion that some things were meant to be. That actions were subject to forces like objects were to gravity.

I think maybe, with the things we do, it's all an illusion, she said. Maybe we don't have any choices. Maybe we're all just helpless.

I was driving. I said, What if I turn here, right now? What if I run us into a telephone pole? I could do it. All it would take would be a flick of the wrist.

But you won't, she said. And if you did, then it was meant to be.

Of course, I didn't buy into that line of horseshit. I've always had problems with that kind of philosophy. I'd had too many fuck-ups, too many mistakes. How do you explain everything I've been through? I said. All those crazy women I've been with? You're telling me they didn't do anything wrong? That I didn't do anything wrong?

Becca reached across the console and put her hand on my knee and squeezed. She said, They got you here, didn't they?

Thinking about all that got me in a terrible way. By the time dinner was ready I was having a hard time getting off the bed because my stomach was churning like mad and I couldn't keep my hands from shaking. It took some time, but I managed and made my way into the kitchen where the table was set with plates and silverware. Becca served the pasta and even got some wine out of the cabinet.

I said. Let's get to it. What's this all about?

Becca nodded and pushed her plate away. She dropped her napkin in the center and the sauce and grease soaked right through. Yeah, she said, taking a breath. Guess we should get to that.

Guess we should, I said.

For a minute or two she sat and fidgeted. Her eyebrow twitched a little. The sunset leaked through the window and cast a pink light on her face.

This is a long time coming, she said. You gotta understand that. You gotta understand I've been fighting this for a while. It's been on my mind every day and I can't shut it up anymore.

All right, I said.

She said, I always tell myself to come out with it. Like, I'm only a couple of days away from telling you. Then I get cold feet and push it off. 'Next week,' I'll say. And then I get scared all over again.

Sure, I said.

But I can't keep doing that, she said. She drummed her fingers on the table and took another drink from her wine.

Part of me wanted to reach for my own glass and gulp it down. I couldn't move though. I kept thinking about Becca pressed against a wall or a cheap motel bed, her body flush and her voice begging for it. I thought of showers and fog-covered mirrors. Damp mattresses and mounds of tangled sheets.

I did something I'm not proud of, she said. And I hope you don't judge me by it.

I said okay.

Cause I love you, she said.

Okay, I said.

I mean, I really love the hell out of you, she said.

I said okay, again.

It was back when I was nineteen, she said. I had so much debt and needed some money.

Okay, I said.

She said, There was this ad in the paper and I got a couple thousand dollars for some pictures.

I asked what kind of pictures.

I don't know, she said. She reached for her wine and knocked the glass over. The few remaining drops spilled on the table as she said, They weren't in good taste.

―――――

I did what any man would do. I got out of my chair and went to her and held her while she cried. She leaned into me, weeping into my chest and gasping for air. She said sorry, sorry, sorry. Over and over. I held her and said it was going to be all right.

It was before you, she said. Before I even knew you were alive.

We left the mess in the kitchen for the morning and made our way to bed. I pulled the covers back and helped her out of her dress. I slipped the thin straps from her shoulders and slid the fabric off her body. We lay together and I stroked the side of her face.

It was such a long time ago, she said, tearing up again. But it's just weighed on me. I didn't want you thinking I'm, some kind of whore or something.

No, I said.

She gritted her teeth and sucked in a stream of air. This has just weighed on me. I mean, I've carried it around for years. I still remember the name of the magazine. The page number and everything.

Becca's eyes flooded. Her body shook as she sobbed and clamped her eyes shut. It was called *Young & Eager*, she said. It was issue number five and I was on pages eighty-one and eighty-two. I don't know why I remember that, she said.

What did they look like? I said. What did they make you do?

She swallowed hard and then gave in to another full-body shiver. She said, I don't want to talk about that.

———

The next morning we got up and she made coffee and cleaned the dishes while I read the paper. Later we made love after we got back from a trip to the store. Becca was fragile then. I touched her softly.

We were watching the evening news on the couch when she moved closer and put her arms around me. She snuck her mouth close to my ear and said thank you for understanding. She said, You're the only one.

After she passed out in bed that night I stayed up a bit. We lived next to one of the main roads in town so traffic was constantly swooshing by. I listened to the cars and they sounded like a breeze and every so often a police car or ambulance would blaze by with their lights and sirens going. I stayed awake listening to them and thinking about the fifth issue of *Young & Eager* magazine.

I tried to picture it, the cover and the pictures inside. Some blonde teenager dressed in a plaid skirt and pigtails on the front, an oversized sucker by her dark red lips. Ads inside for enlargement techniques, pills, and salves. Then maybe some letters about encounters with just-turned-eighteen bombshells. No-strings-attached sex in classrooms and sweaty backseats.

I could see the girls as I flipped through in my mind. No doubt they would be thin and shapely, dressed in coquettish-style clothes and engaged in exaggerated sexual acts. I'd seen these women before. They were dolls caught in a moment of terrible imagination, and their embarrassment was as noticeable as the coating of baby oil shining on their thighs.

After tossing and turning all night I decided I had to know what Becca'd exposed herself to. I had to have that magazine.

I drove to work the next day and paid no attention to traffic or the radio. All I could think about were pages eighty-one and eighty-two. I sat at my desk and signed reports without reading them until it was time for lunch. That's when I drove downtown to the Sugar Shack.

The Shack was an adults-only shop that sat between a pizza place and a broken-down liquor store on Maple Street. Just a small windowless building with a sign that read: The Sugar Shack—Cum On In. It was the kind of place people went to buy lewd favors for bachelorette parties or birthday cards with nudie pictures on them, but there was a curtain that separated the main room from the back and in there were the movies and magazines only perverts wanted to look at.

The guy behind the counter didn't even look up when I came in. The place was empty and smelled like molded rubber. There were toys and novelties on the walls and a few racks of cheap-looking lingerie on the floor. Just past a table of prick-shaped ice cube trays I could see the curtain.

The next room was full of folding tables covered in cardboard boxes. There were posters everywhere of women with large, fake breasts. In the corner, pushed away from the stacks of videos, were the magazines. They felt gummy and filthy to the touch, but I went through every one of them. Unfortunately, the crudely alphabetized selection skipped straight from *Young and Busty* to *Young and Nasty*.

For the next week I called every shop in a fifty-mile radius. Most told me they didn't have it and a handful just hung up on me. I tried calling the publisher, but they'd been shut down for at least six years. Things looked hopeless and I'd pretty much given up on ever getting my hands on a copy. I got frustrated and blew up at Becca over the smallest things. It got so bad I couldn't touch her for fear of what awful things she'd done. I was convinced that every second of every day someone was getting themselves off to her pictures.

It was in May that I finally got a hold of the XXXX Store near Louisville. A man who sounded like he'd had a laryngectomy answered the phone and said, in a fuzzy, mechanical growl, that he had the whole *Young & Eager* series, front to back, and a hundred and fifty would get the complete set or I could pay seven bucks an issue.

I told Becca that night I had business in Kentucky and would leave in the morning. She made tamales and chilled some beer in the freezer. We ate and talked, and laughed for the first time in weeks, but when the dinner was over, and we'd gone to bed, I stopped her from reaching for the waistband of my pajama bottoms.

Stomach's upset, I said.

She sighed and rested her hand on my chest. I think you might be getting an ulcer, she said. You never feel good anymore.

I said maybe and we talked a bit while she settled in, but in my mind I was already showered and shaved, out the door and Kentucky bound.

———

It took seven hours. I stopped once to get some gas and lunch at a station, but couldn't eat for nerves. Whenever I got to seeing signs marking the distance to Louisville I almost veered off the road.

Around four I saw the exit for the XXXX Store. When I got off the ramp there was a billboard for "The Midwest's Largest Selection of Adult Books and Movies." It was a mile down the road, a truck stop full of semis and a little building attached and covered in XXXX signs.

I pulled in and filled my car up and was so nervous I had a hard time working the pump. When it finished I walked to the door and barely had enough strength to pull it open. The inside looked just like every truck stop I'd ever been in. There were aisles and shelves and candy and coolers holding cokes and drinks. Up front was a hot dog cooker and a counter manned by a middle-aged guy wearing a mesh hat and a few days worth of stubble. A half-dozen drivers walked around picking up things

and putting them right back down. Occasionally they'd mean-
der toward the back and into a room marked "The XXXX
Store – Keep Kids Out."

I stared at the sign for a good long time. I knew, a few feet
away from me, was a magazine with my Becca in it, all splayed
out for the world to see. But my legs felt like they would break if
I took even one step toward the room.

Instead, I paid for my gas and asked the cashier where the
closest motel was. He pointed out the window and across the
street. There was a place right there called the Sunset Inn. It
was painted pale yellow and had cable TV. The room was small
and the bed hard, but the set worked just fine. I turned it on and
kicked my feet up.

There was this talk show on. It was about the secrets people
keep from one another. Couple after couple came onto the set
and the tie-wearing host would say, in this awful, sad voice, your
husband, your wife, your lover has something to tell you. One
woman admitted she was a man and hiked up her skirt to show
her shocked boyfriend the evidence. A man with a beard that
crept down his neck told his wife he needed to be chained and
humiliated to find pleasure and a woman entered from offstage
carrying a riding crop and a dog collar. One couple would exit
in tears, only to be replaced by another.

I looked at the phone by the bed and figured I should probably check in with Becca. She answered on the first ring and said
she'd been worried all day. I just had a bad feeling, she said. I can't
explain it. She paused. Anyway. How's Louisville? Is it pretty?

The only thing I could see out the window was the truck
stop and the XXXX Store. A semi was filling up. Diesel was
spilling out of its tank and dripping onto the concrete.

Beautiful, I said.

Becca said Good and laughed a little. I've been thinking about you, she said. Been thinking about you a lot.

Right away I knew where that was heading. Every time I went on business Becca liked to talk a certain way on the phone. It never failed. Her voice would get a little lower and she'd start saying all kinds of racy things.

Is that right? I said. I was tired from the drive, and still upset about the magazine, but a little sweet talk sounded pretty good right then. So I laid back on the bed and got comfortable. Tell me about that, I said.

Well, she said. You know. She laughed a little girl's laugh, an innocent laugh, and I shot right back up. I couldn't handle that laugh. It just served to remind me why I was there in the first place.

She started saying something then, going into detail about what she wanted to do, and I panicked. I did the first thing I could think of. I knocked on the nightstand at my side.

Hey, I said. That's probably my meeting.

What? she said.

My meeting, I said. He said he'd come by when he was ready. I knocked again. That's got to be him, I said.

Oh, Becca said. Well, you better go then. Right?

Right, I said. I'd better go. And I hung up the phone.

I felt awful then and my stomach started hurting. I knew I had to get it over with, that I wouldn't be able to put this whole thing to bed if I didn't find that magazine, so I put my shoes on and walked across the road to the station. There were more men in there, groups of them standing next to the entrance to the XXXX Store, their hands in their pockets and bored looks on their faces. I needed to get myself ready so I stayed away and looked through the candy bars and bags of chips and pork rinds. I pictured myself going in there, finding the magazine and leaving. I tried to talk myself into it.

After putting it off ten or twenty minutes, I walked to the doorway and looked at the sign again. Inside I could see a group of men gathered around a table and I wondered if maybe one of them had found the fifth issue of *Young & Eager* and turned to pages eighty-one and eighty-two.

Look at this one, he might've said.

What do you think about that? another would have said. That's some piece of tail.

I took a step toward them and saw they were looking at a magazine full of women covered in tattoos. Next to them were a few plastic tables holding boxes and boxes of magazines. The ones starting with Y were at the very end of the line where there was a man leafing through in a blue and green flannel and a pair of dry-rotted Levi's. Every couple of seconds he took a handkerchief out of his back pocket and patted his face. I waited him out by going through the box of V-titled books. I skimmed all the way from *Very Big* to *Very Willing* before he took out his handkerchief, blew his nose, and walked away.

I didn't waste any time. I started right in, flipping through dozens of magazines before I found the first issue of *Young & Eager*. On the tattered cover was a girl dressed in a little unbuttoned sailor suit. She was made up to look like she was maybe twelve or thirteen and had big circles of rouge on her cheeks. The next four covers were similar, all with pictures of women done up like dolls and flower girls, one of them dressed in a child's yellow slicker. They were all bursting out of their costumes.

I got to the fifth issue and my chest started hurting. On the front was a brunette girl in the type of pinafore dress Dorothy wore in the Wizard of Oz. Behind her were three men with their pants around their ankles. One had on a flannel like the trucker wore, with a few stalks of straw falling out of his sleeves. The Tin-Man wore a silver funnel atop his head and a toy axe resting over his naked shoulder. The one dressed like the lion looked embarrassed to have a set of cat ears on his head. All three of them had their arms outstretched and a look on their faces that said, Come on, Dorothy. Let's get to this.

I picked the issue out of the box and headed for the line at the counter. There were two fellas ahead of me, each of them with an armload of magazines. They had names like *Lots of Curves* and *Ready for Anything*. The models on the covers looked off the page and stared at me as they spread their legs or sucked on melting popsicles. I paid with a twenty and walked away before I was handed my change.

Back in the room I turned on all the lights and laid the magazine in the middle of the bed. I sat in a chair by the window and looked at it, half-expecting Becca to suddenly appear on the cover. I thought it would be her in that blue and white checked dress, her hair in pigtails, a pair of cheaply made ruby-red flats on her socked feet. But it never changed and I realized I would have to open it to see what there was to see.

So I did. I thumbed through a few ads for pills and phero-mones, straight to a letter from a man who said he'd been giving his daughter's babysitter a ride home when one of the buttons on her shirt popped off and fell into her lap. There were pictures of young girls lying on a picnic blanket in a park. They reached into the wooden basket between them and pulled out pieces of fruit.

I saw the page numbers grow until I reached sixty and I got sick. I made it to the bathroom and hugged the toilet until I'd coughed up everything I'd eaten. On the dirty tile floor I thought of my Becca. I thought of the times spent and secrets told, vows of love that could never be broken. But mostly I thought of her pale skin, the skin that I'd thought had been kept for me and for me alone.

When I got back to the bed the magazine was at pages sixty-seven and sixty-eight. I turned a few more and saw girls wrapped in pink towels across pink beds filled with stuffed animals. They smiled, bright and wide, into the eye of the camera.

I got to pages seventy-nine and eighty and paused. It was a spread of a thin girl hugging the post of her bed. She was smiling but her green eyes were clouded with something. I thought it was regret settling in after hours of shooting for sweaty-faced men. I thought I could see clarity seeping in and building and growing. I stared into them and reached, shaking, to turn the page.

There was a weight there that made me pause, a gravity that stayed my hand. I sat there and pored over it, less than inches from truth and my Becca, a flip of the wrist away, and tried to make myself either turn it or leave it. But I knew right then she was right. About everything. About how the choices didn't matter and we didn't have control. How we were so very helpless.

RESERVATION

I had other things on my mind when Mom called to talk about my brother Larry. Like how I was going to pay that month's bills or how I could keep my marriage from falling apart. Those kinds of things. So I didn't feel bad for not listening too good.

I get it, I told her. Larry's having a hell of a time. Who isn't?

Pat, she said, your baby brother's divorced twice in the last four years and another one just left him. I thought you'd be a little more understanding.

I thought about it a second and realized she might've been right. I looked around where I was standing in my kitchen and saw all the dirty pots and pans sitting in the sink and on the counters. My wife Betty had checked into a hotel a couple of days before and left a hell of a mess behind. Then I realized what Larry was probably going through.

All right, I said into the phone. What do you want me to do?

Do? Mom said. Just call him up. Get him out of the house or something. Be his big brother.

I hung up and grabbed a beer out of the fridge and sucked it down as fast as I could. When it was dry I tossed it in the direction of the trash and watched it bounce off the wall and land on the floor. There was a pile of stuff down there: wrappers and paper plates, coffee grounds, a couple more cans. I didn't feel like cleaning it up and there wasn't anyone around to say anything. I admired the whole thing for a second or two and got back on the phone to call Larry.

He picked up and said hello in the sorriest of voices I'd ever heard.

Hey there, I said. How's everything on that end?

He sighed. You know anything about Indonesia? he asked.

Indonesia? I said.

Yeah, Indonesia.

Can't say I do.

Well, he said, I was talking with a buddy at work and his cousin got him a wife from Indonesia. Said he went over there on a plane and came back with the prettiest little girl. Said she cooks and cleans and never complains.

Ain't that something? I said.

Damn right, he said. Damn right it's something. I could use a change like that, you know? I could really use it.

Neither one of us said anything for a while. There wasn't much to say and we never really talked on the phone very much, so I guess it was a little different. Finally, feeling awkward as hell, I asked him the big question.

I said, So tell me. What happened with Mona? Mona was his wife's name. She was a full-blooded Hopi Indian. Just what went down? I said.

Larry sighed again and I thought I could hear him taking

a long drag off a cigarette. There ain't much to tell, he said. Really not much to it. Things weren't that bad at all. I mean, I thought they were okay. We had fights, sure, but that's the way things go. That's just how it is. But one night I came home from work and she was gone. Took all kinds of shit with her too. The TV, VCR, all the silverware, the blankets and sheets. Hell, she even took Dad's tools.

He stopped talking right then. It was a sore subject. When Dad passed he left his tools to Larry and I didn't get a one of them. It wasn't something we talked about.

I just don't know, he said. Never knew anything like it. Never had someone up and leave and take everything with 'em. Whole deal pisses me off, if you want to know the truth. Just pisses me off to no end.

That's a rotten ass deal, I said.

You said it, he said. You really said it.

Didn't leave a note or anything?

Not a thing. But the bitch of it is I know where she's going. It ain't a secret or anything. She's headed back to her reservation, going back to live with her family.

Where're they? I said.

Arizona, he said. I tell you, if I'd known she was going to pull this shit I wouldn't have said a word to her. Wouldn't have pissed on her if she was on fire. I would've just stayed clear from the very beginning and missed out on a hell of a headache.

There really wasn't much else to say so I got off the phone as soon as I could and grabbed another beer. Like most nights since Betty had left I got me a seat in the living room and watched TV until there wasn't TV to watch anymore. I didn't have work at the time so there wasn't anything to be getting up for in the morning anyway. Had nothing better to do than sit around and drain some beers.

That night I was having a hell of a time falling asleep. Most times I passed out in my recliner and woke up in the middle of the night to head to bed, but I wasn't having any luck. I just kept flipping through the channels over and over and thinking about my brother Larry. I don't know why it was on my mind like it was. I mean, Larry's always had problems with women. They had a way of coming into his life and getting him so excited he couldn't help but propose right off. And what beat all was that each one of them was some different kind of woman.

The first girl was this Mexican he met at work and they were married for all of four months before she got divorce papers. She kept coming back and he kept taking her. They fought all the time. My God, they would fight. Betty and me would go over for dinner every once in a while and they wouldn't even try and hide it. Larry would get up from his chair and check on how the food was coming and before you knew it they'd be just a yelling and calling each other every name in the book. Whole deal lasted two years in all. One day, after having enough I guess, she poured a pot of hot coffee in his lap and walked out the door.

Next one was this religious gal who belonged to some church that said the end of the world was coming. The way Larry explained it she had to buy enough food and things for the two of them to live for seven years after it went down. Made him join the church and everything. Hell, he even had to pay some guys to come and dig out a big concrete hole in his backyard where he could keep the food. She didn't give any more reason for leaving than saying that God had told her it was the right thing to do. What could Larry to say that? What could anyone say to that? Nothing, that's what.

Mona seemed like maybe she'd be different. When he brought her home she was the nicest girl you ever hoped to meet. Red, sure, but kind as the day was long. The first time we met we were all at Mom's house for Sunday supper and Larry brought her in with the biggest of smiles on his face. You could understand why just by looking. Those injun' genes had been good to her. She had this long black hair that shined in the light and these really sharp features you couldn't help but stare at. And whenever Mom brought out the chicken and biscuits Mona couldn't stop thanking her. She was just what the doctor ordered for my baby brother.

After Betty and me left supper that night we couldn't stop talking about how great it was that Larry had found him a woman like Mona. We were driving home and Betty kept saying how pretty and nice she was, how she'd been praying for a long time that Larry'd find someone sweet and kind and pretty and how it'd finally come to pass. I didn't know about that. I mean, I thought she was great, but I wasn't about to get all out of sorts over her.

Let's not get our hopes up, I said to Betty. God knows he's had a hell of a time trying to keep a girl around.

What's that supposed to mean? she said, raising her voice. You don't give Larry enough credit. These other women weren't anything but trouble. Bunch of crazies who tried to ruin his life. I can already tell this one's different. I can just tell.

I said I didn't know yet. He's just a fuck-up, I said. Lord knows he'll figure out some way to mess this whole thing up. He always does, I said.

Betty got all fired up over that. Patrick, she said. I want you to know I think you're a good man, but you don't support your brother the very least bit. I mean, who needs enemies with a brother like you?

Honest, I don't know how I answered that. I probably turned up the radio or something. For all I know I rolled down the window and stuck my head out in the breeze. But sitting there in my living room and thinking about the whole thing made me feel awful. I kept thinking about what Betty had said and about all the things she'd said in the past. I realized she'd been right most of the time. Hell, all the time. And here I was, lazing around my dirty home without her. I was some kind of mess.

The whole deal got to me. I got to feeling bad about Larry and his problems so I called him again. It was about three in the morning, so it took some time before he picked up. I just let it ring. Probably two dozen times before he answered. He sounded tired and sore as hell.

What the fuck? he said. Who's calling after three in the goddamn morning?

I said, "You know where Mona's going right? You know where she's from and all that stuff?

Sure, he said.

Tell you what. How'd you like to go and get your shit back? Huh? he said.

How'd you like to go and get your TV and VCR and all Dad's tools?

How? he asked.

Tell you what, I said, grabbing another beer from the icebox. You get a couple days off work and we'll head on out west. We'll be in 'Zona before you know it and we'll find that bitch.

We'll find her surer than shit.

Yeah?

Yeah.

When I hung up I was feeling so good and drunk that I turned on the radio in the living room and found a station playing some good ol' rock 'n roll. I turned it up loud and started dancing around the house. Every one of those songs sounded so good I couldn't help but jive around the place. Then some Eagles came on and made me think of when Betty and me started dating. We used to meet up at this bar downtown called Parrot's and we'd dance all night to the songs on the jukebox. She loved the Eagles and though I didn't care much for them I danced right along with her. Those were some good times, I tell you.

All of that led to me picking up the phone again and dialing up the hotel where she was staying. It was this little drive-up place a couple of towns over and I had the number circled in the phonebook. I got the front desk and some lady answered. She directed the call to Betty's room and it rang and rang. I figured she was probably asleep. I mean, that woman would sleep through a hurricane if you let her. Finally the answering machine kicked in and I started leaving a message. I told her about Larry and Mona and how she'd stolen all his things and headed out west. How we were going to be hot on her tail and how I was helping my little brother out, just like she wanted. I told her everything that was on my mind, everything about the pots and the pans, the trash on the floor, and the Eagles on the radio. I told her I'd be calling soon and that I missed her. That I always missed her.

We started off, Larry and me, on a dark Tuesday morning. It was already raining buckets by six and didn't look to let up anytime soon, so we stopped into a gas station at the edge of town and filled up and got some coffee. From there we drove west and sipped our coffees and didn't talk or do much at all. Larry tried flipping on the radio but we were driving in my old Chevy pickup and it had a habit of coming in as nothing but static. After a half hour or so of jockeying he gave up and clicked it off.

It didn't take long for me to regret the trip. I mean, by the time we hit Illinois I couldn't believe we were doing it. Neither Larry or me really had anything to talk about and the silence in the cab was terrible. I was too busy trying to think of something to say to my brother to even pay attention to the lines on the road. We tried talking baseball but he didn't give a damn for the game and when he started telling me about work I realized I couldn't care less what a welder does. Around Kansas City I had serious thoughts about turning around and just heading home. I knew we still had a couple of days' worth of driving ahead of us and the prospect sounded awful.

The first night we parked at a rest stop outside of Topeka and tried to get an hour or two of sleep. It wasn't that bad out so we rolled down the windows to let the air in. I'd brought along a couple of sixers and we drank some beers and tried to relax. I don't know about Larry but I got about ten minutes of shuteye before the sun came up and blazed through the windshield. A candy bar or two out of the machines inside and we were off.

The silence didn't stop. It got so bad I started singing some nonsense song I'd heard somewhere and banging out the rhythm on the steering wheel. I could tell Larry felt it too because he tried again with that radio. He didn't have any kind of luck and when he turned it off he clapped his hands and looked at me.

You know what the worst part of all of it is? he said. You know what really chaps my ass about Mona up and leaving?

What's that? I said.

Well, he said, I'll tell you. The week before she took off was probably the best week of my life. One of those weeks where you can't help but get along with your woman. Everything's just coming together. Dinner tastes better than ever, beer's colder, and the both of you just walk around with these dopey-ass smiles on your faces. You know?

I said sure.

That Thursday before she left we were in bed, he said, rolling down his window and pushing his hand outside. He pressed against the wind like a little kid likes to do and glided his hand up and down. And we were just laying there talking about the future. About having a baby and things like that. We were wanting a family and then she leaves like she does. I can't help but wonder if she was lying to me. But why would she do that? Why tell someone you want to have kids if you don't want to?

I don't know, I said.

Me either, he said. I don't know. I just don't know for shit. A guy wakes up in the morning and thinks he knows anything, he doesn't know jack. That's just the way it is. Someday I'm gonna have to face it and man up to the fact I don't know anything.

I don't think anyone does, I said. I know I sure as hell don't. Look at Betty and me. I mean, I thought we had a real good thing going and then it's gone. Just gone. And I've tried asking just what the hell happened, or what's going on, and she won't say a word. That's how it goes. I tell you, that's really how it goes.

Well, Larry said, I'll tell you one thing. One thing I damn well know. We get there and we find Mona? I'm gonna give her a piece of my mind. That's just what I'm going to do. I'm going to say 'Listen here,' and just lay into her. Let her know just how goddamn awful it is to come home to an empty house. Let her know just what I think about her and her thieving ways.

Good, I said.

Yep, said Larry. He lit up a cigarette and put his feet out the truck's window and leaned back. He looked real happy with himself. I'm going to tell that little lady exactly what I think about her and her kind and that's that. Yep, that's that, he said.

The landscape started changing when we got around New Mexico. There were more hills and the dirt turned red. Then there were these big rocks everywhere. We stopped in a little town surrounded by cliffs and plateaus and took some pictures. Larry and me were laughing about how everyone back home was going to be shocked when they saw them. To celebrate our good times we got lunch at a diner and ordered plates full of fries and hamburgers and chicken-fried steak. I told the waitress I wanted a strawberry milkshake and got up to make a call. I figured Betty would want to hear about our little trip and things I'd been seeing.

Hello? she answered. Hello?

Hi there, I said. Hey it's Pat. You get my message the other day?

Pat? she said. How'd you get this number? How'd you get a hold of this number?

The front desk, I said. I couldn't figure out why she was so unhappy to hear from me. I mean, I figured at worst she'd be happy to hear from me. But it seemed just the opposite.

Okay, she said, starting to sound annoyed. Patrick, you can't call me here all right? You've got to leave me alone and get over this thing.

No, no, I said. Larry and me are in New Mexico. We're heading out to find Mona. You remember her right? She took off with everything he owned—

–That's fine, that's fine. Just leave me alone, all right?

Why Betty? I said. Then I heard another voice in the room. I thought for sure it sounded like a man's voice. Who's that? I said. Who's that in the room?

No one, she said. Get off here, okay? Go take care of your brother or whatever. Just don't call again. Don't call. And she hung up.

When I got back to the table it was covered with all sorts of food and Larry was smiling from ear to ear. He had a fork in his hand and he was holding it like a knife and using it to stab at the food laid out in front of him. For the first time in months he looked happy.

What's your deal? I said.

I don't know, he said and took a big bite of scrambled eggs. Just been feeling so small lately. You know how that is? Like life could just step on you any second?

I said yeah.

I've been feeling like that for the longest time, he said. Every day I've ever lived I've felt like that. He took a second and pushed around his food with his fork. This has got to be the best idea you've ever had, Pat. It has to be. No one's ever done something like this for me. No one. I mean, giving that bitch Mona a piece of my mind is gonna really do it for me. It's really going to help with everything.

I said good and that I was glad to hear it.

After we ate we got back on the road and inched closer and closer to Arizona. The rocks rose up like they were welcoming us in. By the time we reached the state limit the sun had set and we were speeding down the highway and into the desert. All around, for as far as you could see, was a mix of pitch black and this weird blue that hovered above the ground. For hours at a time there wasn't anyone else on the road, just the occasional car abandoned on the shoulder. It was quiet and beautiful and when Larry tried the radio again it came alive with perfect reception. We listened to rock 'n roll and country and even some old Mexican songs. We laughed and smoked and it was hard to tell if I was still driving or dreaming. I couldn't help but think of Betty and what she'd said.

In the morning the sun came out and we saw we'd crossed into a reservation. A sign on the side of the road labeled it Navajo ground. We saw people walking by in T-shirts and jeans with holes in them. There were mobile homes scattered all over the place with lines of wash drying in the sun. A store here and there falling apart. There were little kids tossing baseballs back and forth in gravel lots and chasing them whenever they got loose. I asked Larry if any of it looked like what he thought it would. He told me no and I told him it didn't to me either.

The Hopi's plot sits right in the heart of the Navajo land and it took a solid two hours to get there. When we did we found more of the same. There were still mobile homes parked everywhere and kids wandering around dressed like any regular kids. We pulled up alongside a group and asked where we could find the Woods'. That was Mona's family. Those kids hopped up into the bed of my truck and told me the way. When we pulled up in front of this old modular with gray panels and red shutters, they told us we were there.

Larry and me got out of the truck and took the place in. The lot was mostly just dirt and dust and there were a few broken-down cars parked next to the modular. A couple had their hoods up and a couple more were up on blocks. That place looked like a real dump, I tell you. No place I'd want to live, that's for sure.

I followed my brother up the steps to the front door and waited as he knocked. The kids who'd shown us the way were standing around my truck and lighting up cigarettes and passing them around. There were three of them, the oldest being maybe thirteen, and they seemed curious as hell as to what a couple of white men were doing knocking on doors. I watched them to make sure they weren't going to get to snooping in my truck. I'd brought along a piece and had it in the glove box in case Larry and me ran into trouble with the Woods. Last thing I needed was some Indian kid breaking in and pawning off my revolver.

I was watching them real close until the door opened and I saw an old Indian standing in the doorway. He didn't have a hair on his head and you could tell by the look on his face he was real sick with cancer or something like it. He had a blanket wrapped around him and the hand holding onto the doorknob was shaking real bad.

Yeah? he said.

Yeah, Larry said. Mona Wood live around here?

The old man nodded and coughed into his fist. He opened the door and motioned for us to come inside. The first room we walked into was the living room and it wasn't anything to get excited over. There was an old beat-up couch with tears in the pillows and some blankets on the walls. In the corner was a tray with a television on it. It didn't take very long to figure out it was the TV Mona had taken from my brother. On the floor right next to it was Dad's box of tools.

The old man settled down on the couch and took a deep breath. You know Mona? he said.

I'm her husband, Larry said. I'm the guy Mona married.

Oh, the old man said. You're the guy Mona married. He took a sip of water from a glass that was sitting on a stand next to the couch and wiped his mouth with the back of his hand. Oh, he said again.

Is she around? Larry said.

Work, the old man said. Work right now. Hold on, he said. Hold on. Then he yelled and got to coughing and carrying on and had to start drinking from that water again. In a couple of seconds a kid came running. He looked just like all the kids we'd been seeing all morning. The old man told the boy to get some seats and he came back with a couple of metal folding chairs from the next room. He handed them to us and disappeared back to where he came from.

Larry and I had a seat in those chairs. We sat down in that living room and waited for Mona to come home from work.

Turn it on, the old man said.

What's that? Larry said.

The old man pointed at the television on the tray, Larry's television, and told him to turn it on. Larry pressed a button and the screen came alive. The show that was on was about a construction company building a big skyscraper in New York. They had on hard hats and kept unrolling these big old blueprints. Then there were scenes of guys putting down girders and bolting them together. After them came the welders and Larry said aloud to no one in particular that that was the kind of stuff he did for a living. The old man smiled and nodded, but I'm not sure he knew what was being said anyway. We kept on watching that show. Kept on watching as they put together this building that grew and grew in the New York skyline until it towered over all the other huge buildings around it.

We were really getting into that show, I know I was anyway, when the door opened and in came Mona. She looked just like I remembered her from the supper at Mom's house and I couldn't help but wave hello to her. She saw Larry and froze up. She stood there in the doorway for a good long time and just looked at us. Then the old man said something and she finally closed the door.

Hi Larry, she said. She went and put her purse in the kitchen and came back in and sat down next to the old man. She had on an olive green dress that looked like maybe she was waitressing or something. She looked scared to death.

Hi there, my brother said.

After a couple of minutes she got back up and asked if Larry would come with her into the kitchen while she made dinner. I watched them walk in together to the next room and I was left in front of the TV with the old man. We didn't talk. We just watched that show some more. We watched the men with their tools and their hard hats building this skyscraper. Pretty soon its frame was finished. It looked like a huge gray skeleton. Then more men came and started putting in these big windows. I mean, these windows alone were probably bigger than the living room we were sitting in. I couldn't believe it, really. I was so surprised to see windows that big that I looked over to the old man to see if he was surprised too, but he looked the same as when he answered the door.

The whole time we were watching that show you could hear voices getting a little louder every once in a while in the kitchen. I think Larry and Mona were getting into it a little bit, like they were getting upset. I thought I heard my brother ask how she could do something like that to him, but I could be wrong. At one point there was crying I think. Then silence and the sound of something hissing.

We sat at the table in the kitchen for dinner. It was a cramped space so there wasn't much room to move around or get comfortable. Mona got a pot off the stove and put it in the middle of the table. It was some kind of bean soup and there was fresh bread on a plate next to it. For a while we just ate. Larry and me couldn't get enough of the stuff. We had all kinds of bread and kept spooning big spoonfuls of the soup. It was simple, but it was the best thing I'd had in a real long time. Thinking about it now I can almost taste it. I slowed down after a while though because Mona and the old man were taking their time and savoring each bite. They were measuring their bowls and sipping tiny sips.

All in all it was a hell of a time until the old man started coughing again and doubled over in his seat. He sat there hacking and carrying on, his body folded up and convulsing. Neither one of us knew what to do and just watched as Mona helped the old man up and carried him out of the room. Larry and me sat there and waited. We didn't know if we should go and help. After a bit Mona came back and she had that little kid from earlier with her. The kid sat down in the old man's chair and started slurping at the soup.

My dad is sick, Mona said. I'm sorry.

Larry told her it wasn't a problem and went back to eating.

When we finished dinner Larry helped Mona wash the dishes and I took up in the living room again. The show that had been on the television wasn't on anymore and all I could make out through the screenful of snow was some kind of parade. I could see some floats and smiling cheerleaders and baton twirlers, but then they'd be gone, passed over in an ocean of static. I slapped the side of the TV and the picture came back, but then it left again.

My brother came in from the kitchen and asked me to get the truck heated up. I almost asked what the rush was or what'd happened, but I saw by the look on his face that it wasn't time to ask any questions. So I turned off the TV and went outside and started the truck. With the exception of a few streetlights here and there the night was almost as dark as it'd been out in the desert.

Larry got in a little while later. He opened up the driver's side door and told me to scoot over. Told me he'd take the first leg of driving back home. Said he felt that good. That he just wanted to drive and drive through the night. When he got in he plopped something down on the seat between us. I reached over and touched it and felt the smooth, cold metal. I knew then he'd at least gotten Dad's toolbox back and it was just about the best feeling ever.

It was so nice and peaceful that I leaned back and tried to catch a few minutes of sleep. I got real comfortable and felt that bean soup sitting in my stomach all nice and warm and couldn't help but smile. For a minute I tried to watch the scenery go by, but it was too dark to see much of anything. I started thinking about Betty and that got me sad again. I thought of our dark house where she wasn't waiting for me, and that hotel room where she was staying. I thought about the voice I'd heard.

But then I let it pass. I touched the toolbox again. All I could see, there in the truck, was that building on the television. That building climbing up toward the sky. The girders dull and tired in the morning light and the windows sparkling against the sun. I thought of myself standing on the very top of that building and looking out over everything. I thought about standing up there, as wide and tall as the world.

OLD TIMES

Albie Jensen was talking about what made him stop drinking in the first place. That's what we talked about, what with us being stuck in the facility due to all the rain.

I was coming home from this bar called the Oodle Inn, he said. Had the windows rolled down and the air turned on full blast. I was so drunk I would've passed out if I didn't. I mean, I was blitzed to the point of blacking right out.

We sat in a circle, the boys and me, and took turns bullshitting. There wasn't much to do otherwise, 'cept for maybe play cards or take a walk by the river over yonder, but you get tired of euchre after so many hands and the rain hadn't let up for five days.

Thing is, Albie said, I put her in gear and I'm talking to God. Well, maybe not God, but the universe, and I'm sayin', 'Get me home. Get me home safe and I won't touch another drop for the rest of my life.' Making a deal, y'know? And I get out on the road, just a few blocks from my street, and I pull up to a red light and it just won't change.

I'd heard that story a dozen times if I heard it once. Just like I'd heard Pat tell how he'd checked himself in after he nearly beat his girl to death with a head full of gin and tonics. Or, how Truck knew he had a problem when he woke up from a bender in a gas station in Kentucky, not knowing where he was or how he got there. I knew those stories so well I could've told 'em myself.

And I'm sitting at that light, Albie said, putting his hands up like he had a hold of a wheel. He was a big man and had a great big set of paws on him. I knew it was gonna happen, he said. But I was still surprised when those red and blue lights switched on.

That's the part of the story that always got me nervous. No drunk worth his weight in booze doesn't know the feeling of getting a cop on his bumper after knocking a few down. God knows I've shook a tail or two, but right then, what with the cabin fever and all, I got antsy and started looking out the window. The rain was coming down hard and the ground was already giving way to big ponds of water.

I asked the guys. I said, You reckon that river's gonna flood? It was a valid question, what with Charlie Gillen, the facility's head honcho, running out there to check its level every hour.

I don't know, Truck said. It's anybody's guess.

No doubt about it, Pat said, pulling a cigarette from his shirt pocket. He raised it shakily to his lips and lit it after struggling with the lighter. Sure as God made little green apples that thing's gonna flood.

Can I finish my story? Albie said, flustered. Can I tell my damn story?

Tell your story, Pat said and took a drag from his cigarette. Don't make a bit of difference though, cause that river's gonna flood and that water's heading this-a-way.

Can I tell my story? Albie said, again.

Tell your story, Truck said.

I don't remember where I was, Albie said.

You were about to be pulled over by the sheriff, I told him. You were about to try and buy him off and he was about ready to throw your drunk ass in jail.

That's right, Albie said.

He went on to tell the rest of his story, the same way he always told it. He talked about fumbling to get his license out of his wallet and sliding in a twenty dollar bill as he handed it over to the sheriff. He talked about how the sheriff threw it on the hood of his car and dragged him out and into the street. And then he went on and on about how his wife came down to bail him out and how sad she looked the whole way home, but I wasn't listening. Not really, anyway.

I was thinking about the river out there. It'd been the one place I could go at the facility to get a little peace and quiet. After I checked myself in I wandered up to the levy one day and found it lazing along, a gray sheet of water just taking its time. It wasn't huge at that point, it wasn't anything to look at really, but there was something nice and calm about it. Pretty soon I was going down there all the time for a walk or run. Got in pretty good shape, what with all that exercise.

Course, it was a change from the life I'd been leading up to that point. Since I'd met Lisa I'd been carrying on like I wanted to kill myself. The two of us meshed like fire and air and fed off each other. One of us would get to drinking and the other would follow suit. Before we hooked up we both had jobs, her at the grocery and me down at the factory, but it didn't take long for that to change. Soon we were both canned and using our unemployment to keep us floating in booze.

There were days there where we drank from sunup to sundown. One of us would drive over to the Shop N Save, where Lisa'd worked before getting fired, and pick up a bottle or two of cheap red wine and either a handle of vodka or a fifth of whiskey. Then we'd sit on the couch and drink and fight and watch whatever came on the TV. Most of the time it was soap operas or talk shows and we'd scream at the set like those actors and poor bastards could hear us.

Truck said, What about you, Frank? I guess Albie had finished his story. What got you in here?

I borrowed a cigarette off Pat and settled in my chair. I told 'em about Lisa and me. I told 'em about how one day we were watching this soap opera where everyone who'd ever died on the show came back to life. It was like nothing had ever changed and everyone just went about their business as if they'd never died at all. And I told them about the commercial that came on, the one for the pound, and how it showed all these animals in cages and that really got to Lisa. She was soft like that, and she said, right away, we got to go get us a pet, a dog or a cat or something. And we did. We went and got this mutt, this real sad-looking thing with matted hair and bloodshot eyes. We got it and took it home and went out and bought some food and bowls and toys at the Shop N Save. We even got some fancy rum to celebrate.

What kind of rum? Pat said. I told him I didn't remember. It'd been a while. I like rum, he said. I like rum in coke and I like rum all by itself. Makes your stomach warm.

Well, I said, we drank the fancy rum and played with that mutt all night. Tossed a ball across the floor and it'd go and get it and bring it right back. I don't think I ever saw Lisa happier, I said.

That's a good dog, Truck said.

Those are the best kind, Pat added. They'd do anything for you.

It didn't want anything else in the world, I said. Just for us to throw that ball again and again.

Then I got to the point in the story that I hated telling. The part where we finished off that rum and a six-pack of beer that'd been left in the fridge. I told them how Lisa'd gone in the bedroom while I played with that mutt, and how I'd thought she was in there on the phone with her ex-husband Mike again.

I just knew, I said. Every couple of nights she'd call him up and get to talking about how sorry she was and how she'd messed up bad and all she wanted in the world was for things to be like they used to be. Well, I said, I beat on the door and told her to come out. But she wouldn't. She stayed in there and I got to the point where I thought I heard voices.

So, I said, I did the only thing that made sense at the time. I picked up that mutt, the same one she'd been playing with and falling in love with all night, and I tossed it out the goddamn door. Kicked at him 'til he ran off.

That's a shame, Albie said.

It is, Truck said.

I agreed, but I didn't say so. I didn't want to talk anymore. I didn't feel like saying how Lisa and me had it out after that and broke nearly everything in the house, or how I woke up the next morning, hungover as hell and even more ashamed, and how I went out into the neighborhood to look for that mutt but couldn't find him. I didn't want to think about Lisa slunk down in a chair covered in cigarette burns, her eyes red and face pale, her toes tracing the rim of a dirty dog bowl. All I wanted to think about right then was the river and its water and all that rain and weight mixing out there in the dark.

━━━━

That morning Charlie Gillen woke everybody at five-thirty and told us to get dressed. The river had jumped the levy and he needed every man out there to help with sandbags. We threw on our boots and went out into the cold rain. Already the water was rushing down the hill and mixing with all the puddles and mud. It was all we could do just to walk.

For four hours we fought that river back. Truck and Pat and some other boys shoveled the sand and Albie and me tried to stack those bags the best we could. There must've been two dozen of us, Charlie and his staff included, but there wasn't no stopping that river. The water snuck through the cracks in some places and just climbed up and over in others. By ten we were back at the facility, packing our things and making calls for rides.

Pat said to hell with it. He took his suitcase and walked in the direction of town. Didn't have an umbrella or anything. Just took right off.

That left Albie, Truck, me, and a few other fellas to wait in the main den. We tried to get a quick card game going, but no one seemed interested. All anyone wanted to do was stand by the window and watch the river flood down the hill. That seemed as good of an idea as any, so I put the cards away and joined them.

Truck was the next to go. Charlie Gillen and him knew each other a bit, so he offered him a ride. The two of them packed into his lime-green Chevy and motored out of there. That left me and Albie to hold down the fort.

Albie told me he hadn't seen his wife since his court date and I asked him if they'd talked at all. No, we ain't, he said. She told me that day, she said, 'Honey, don't you call 'til you're cured. Don't you dare call 'til you're all the way better.' And that's what I said to her this morning. I said, 'Baby, I'm as cured as cured can be.'

Pretty soon a blue station wagon pulled up in the parking lot. Now, I'd never spent much time picturing what a woman who'd marry a guy like Albie would look like, but if I had I bet I would've imagined her just like this girl. She was kind of big, round almost, and she looked plain. She had this plastic on her hair, so I couldn't get too close a look, but she was plain, I could tell that. She got out of that car and splashed her way up the steps to the door and ducked inside. Albie said goodbye to me and met her there. I watched him and his round, plain wife run out to the car together, arm in arm, and I watched him open her door and slide behind the wheel. As they were pulling away I noticed, for the first time, a set of hands and a child's face pressed against the back window. The glass was fogged, but I could see they belonged to a plain-looking little boy with a mop of black hair.

After they left it was just me by my lonesome. For a while I sat in the den and watched the river some more. The water was picking up steam at that point, running down the hill and turning the facility's backyard into a swamp. Those sandbags we'd stacked were scattered all over the place. They looked like rocks out there.

I picked up the phone to call someone, but I remembered I didn't really have anyone to call. Both my folks were dead and I'd lost every friend I'd ever had when Lisa and me got to drinking heavy. I thought about giving her a ring, but I figured she probably didn't want anything to do with me. It'd only been two months since everything had gone sour and I didn't reckon that was enough time to heal all the hard feelings she had.

So I put down the phone and made myself comfortable. I figured I had another day or so until the flood got inside the facility and I wasn't in a hurry. Hell, I didn't care right then if the water were to sweep in and drown me. That sounded good, all things considering. It sounded like a pretty decent way to go.

In the kitchen I got some cold cuts out of the fridge and made a sandwich. I poured myself a glass of milk and had a little lunch in the den. I even pulled a chair up to the window so I could watch the flood. It was like having a front row seat to a big concert, only the show was a bunch of muddy water trickling around some sandbags and down a sopping wet hill.

I noticed the patch I'd ran along had washed out already. It figured, considering it was just a thin strip of dirt that ran along the top of the levy. That made me sad though, seeing that path gone. I'd walked or ran that thing every day for at least a month. Got to know it pretty well, too. Of all the things I could do at the facility, watching TV or sitting around bullshitting, the only thing that didn't make me think about drinking was running down that path.

That was silly though. Getting all upset over a path like that. Acting like I didn't care if I got drowned in a flood or not. I came to my senses and got on the horn. I called up Lisa and hoped the phone hadn't been disconnected.

It rang about twenty times and I started wondering if I should hang up. But finally she answered. Hello, she said. Who is it?

It's Frank, I said. I need to be picked up.

Frank, she said. What do you mean?

I need to be picked up, I said. At the facility.

For some reason it took her a while to process what I was saying. I told her about the flood and the path and everything and even then she didn't quite understand.

Wait, she said. You need to be picked up?

I do, I said.

At the facility?

At the facility, I said.

Okay, she said. Okay. And she hung up the phone.

The facility was a forty-minute drive from our house, so I figured, with short notice, it'd take about an hour or so for Lisa to get there. She'd need to freshen up, I guessed, and she'd probably need to get dressed and put some makeup on. Maybe she'd even put some gas in the car. It'd take an hour and a half, tops. But, by the time she pulled up, two hours had slipped by.

I was waiting on the front steps when she did. The rain was still coming down and the car sent big splashes of water out as it rolled through. There were dents and scrapes up and down the driver's side. The side mirror was gone and there were some loose wires sprouting out of the opening like wild hairs. I ran through the rain and jumped in the passenger door. I was soaked at that point, my clothes and hair wet like I'd just stepped out of the shower. I wiped my face and looked at her, at my Lisa.

She looked tired. That's what I remember. It was like she was having a hard time just keeping her eyes open. But she was just as beautiful as I'd ever seen her. She had her hair down and some mascara on her lashes. All in all, it was probably the most tired and most beautiful she'd ever looked.

Hi, I said, not knowing anything else to say. How're you, honey? How're you?

Without saying anything she leaned in and kissed me hard on the mouth. I kissed her back, like we were picking up right where we left off. We kissed like that, in the car, the rain thumping on the roof and windshield, we kissed like that for a long, long time. We took turns touching each other and I tasted cigarettes and wine on her breath. It was enough to put a charge in me, like touching a live wire, and all I wanted was to get my hands on a bottle of sweet red.

After a while we pulled apart and Lisa drove us away from the facility. As she did she told me everything she'd been doing for the past two months. I put my hand on her thigh and listened. She told me how back home the power was off but it'd be turned back on Thursday after a check cleared the bank. She told me about a friend she'd made, a widow named Darla who she met at the Shop N Save in the liquor aisle. They'd been drinking and watching the soap operas together since I'd checked myself in.

That's where I scraped up the car, Lisa said. I was pulling out of Darla's driveway. It's real long and surrounded by trees, you know, and I'd had some old fashioneds, and I guess I clipped one on my way out.

I reckon so, I said, squeezing her leg. It was so good seeing her I didn't care about anything.

And there were these people watching, she said. Her neighbors were all out in their yard, this whole big family with kids and everything. They were all out there playing baseball or something. Lisa slapped her forehead. I hit that tree and everyone looks up, she said. They all watched and it was scraping so loud. I could've died, it was so embarrassing.

I said it was okay and touched her shoulder. Who cares? I said. I mean, who really cares?

Lisa smiled. Listen, she said. There's this little place around here. My dad used to talk about it all the time. It's called Noonan's. They've got the best chicken you've ever had.

I thought about it. After two months of eating lousy TV-dinners at the facility, some fried chicken sounded like it would hit just the spot.

Yeah, I said. Sounds good. But can we make a stop? I'm feeling a bit out of sorts.

Sure, she said and pulled into the next gas station. I ran in and went straight to the beer cooler in the back. I got a couple of cases and a bottle of wine, just like I'd wanted. The cashier tried to talk to me about the rain, but all I was interested in was a bottle opener.

That's a good one, Lisa said when I got in the car and got to work uncorking the wine. That's a real good one, if I do say so myself.

There wasn't much in the way of proper glasses in the car, so we made due with some old drive-thru cups rolling round in the backseat. I poured them full and gave Lisa one.

What should we toast to? she said. You coming home? Health?

How about old times? I said, nudging her cup with mine.

I like that, she said with a smile. To old times.

That first drink went down smoother than any before it. It ran down my throat and it felt like the whole world had had a fresh coat of paint thrown on. Lisa got us back on the road and in no time the two of us were laughing about the past and making plans for the future. We thought maybe a move would do us good. Maybe we could scrape together a little money and make a brand new start of it in Indianapolis. We had relations up there, after all. It was an option.

Do you remember, she said, that time we drove there to see my sister?

Of course I did. That wasn't the type of thing someone forgets. We'd been invited up for Thanksgiving and I didn't want to go in the first place. Lisa was worried though, worried that if we didn't her sister would never talk to her again. That was right around when things with us and our drinking were getting out of hand and we couldn't afford to lose anybody else.

We made it to Indy, she said, sauced out of our minds. God knows how.

You were driving like crazy, I said, finishing my drink. Swerving and cutting people off.

I wasn't that bad, she said.

I said, You were. You almost killed us merging onto 465. You didn't check your mirrors. You just went.

And then we just kept going round that big circle, she said. We kept missing the exit. Over and over and over again. She laughed. We got there though. You've got to give me that.

Six hours later, I said. I got a beer for the each of us out of the case in the backseat. Long enough so that all we could do was go to bed when we got there and get up and leave in the morning.

Oh God" she said. I know.

We didn't even get to see the kids. We just had some coffee and toast and had to drive again.

We laughed about that for a while. Things seemed good, the two of us together. I remember thinking about how we were still in love and that got me feeling better than I'd felt in a long time. The rain even let off. It slowed down 'til it stopped and the sun peeked out.

The rest of the drive over to Noonan's we laughed some more and polished off that bottle of wine. Everything looked different. The farms and their fields were all flooded to hell. Big lakes of shimmering water surrounded houses and barns and turned them into little islands. The water came right up to the road and threatened to spill over.

It's damn good seeing you, Lisa said at one point. I didn't know what to expect, not having seen you in a while and all.

Damn good seeing you, I said to her and gave her shoulder a little squeeze.

She leaned over, keeping the wheel straight with her hands, and laid a good, long kiss on me. When she pulled away she said she wanted a new start. She said, I want to put everything in the past. I want to just let go of all the baggage. Give this thing a real shot.

That's what I want, I said and leaned into her. That's all I'd wanted to hear in forever. By the time I checked into the facility we'd had a ton of that baggage. Fighting every day for a year will do that. You start collecting everything the other person's ever done wrong. You start keeping score, is what you do.

You mean it? she said, starting to cry a little bit. She drummed the steering wheel and smiled. You mean drop everything?

Everything, I said.

Honey, she said. That's just the best thing I've ever heard. I'm so glad.

Me too, I said. I leaned across the console and got as close to her as I could. Thank you, I said.

———

Noonan's was a mile or two down the road. It was this shack-looking bar with a couple of trucks and a half-dozen tractors parked in the lot. The flood had come right up to the ditch behind it, giving the bar a riverside view. The metal walls were rusted and the windows covered with trash bags.

It looks rough, Lisa said, leading me up to the door. But it's really not. I swear, she said.

She wasn't lying. The only people inside were a bunch of sunburned farmers watching a ballgame on a black and white TV behind the bar. We grabbed a table in the back and a woman with the longest red hair I'd ever seen came over and got our orders. She twirled that long red hair with her pen as we ordered some chicken and beer. She brought out the beer and some bread and slaw to tide us over.

Jesus, I said, taking a swig, I missed beer.

Lisa popped hers open and lit herself a cigarette. I can imagine, she said.

We talked a little bit about the look of the place and how her dad would come in there with his buddies after a day of hunting. He was always telling her and her family about the deer and boar heads on the walls. He said everywhere you looked there was either some kind of head or bird or something. And he always talked about the farmers who'd be sitting at the bar. Didn't matter what time of day they came in, there'd always be the same line of guys sitting there watching the TV.

We joked that maybe those were the same old timers up there, the same ones who'd been there when her dad and his friends came in. We laughed about that a little while and then Lisa said she needed to say something. She took a big gulp of beer and said, I just want to say, I'm happy we talked today. I mean, I'm happy you called me, but I'm more happy it's gone like this. I've spent the better part of the last two months trying not to love you, Frank, and I didn't know what to do. It's just a relief, she said, to be back in this thing and getting over the old stuff.

I know, I said. I'm real happy about it, too.

I mean, she said, there was a lot to get over. That red-haired girl brought us each out a basket full of fried chicken and another beer. Lisa said thank you and started picking at one of the pieces. It's just been hard, she said, this whole thing. Being in love and being so angry.

It wasn't easy, I said. I finished my first beer and opened my second. I said I had some stuff to get over too. That I had some things I had to stew over.

I guess, she said. She ate for a while and then looked across the table. I just think what I had to deal with was pretty bad. That's all.

We both screwed up, I said.

We ate and drank. That chicken was mighty good and the more I ate the more I wanted to drink. That waitress with the red hair kept up with us, bringing out fresh cans and extra pieces when we asked for them. She'd come over and pick up our trash and smile real big like she was so happy we were there. Looks like ya'll are hungry, she said, and added, That's good. I like hungry people.

I was getting a pretty heavy buzz on. It'd been a while since I'd drank and I was trying to make up for lost time. All that beer got me thinking about things. Lisa was saying something, God knows what, maybe something about laundry for all I know, and I couldn't help but to say it.

I said, The least you could've done was hide the calls.

What? Lisa said. Hide what calls?

To Mike, I said. You could've at least tried to hide it.

Hide what? she said. I don't have to hide anything.

You used to get liquored up, I said. You'd get liquored up and go in the bedroom and call Mike. I heard you, I said.

She was holding a piece of bread in her hand and she dropped it into an empty basket. You're out of your goddamn mind, she said.

Bullshit, I said. You'd sneak in there and call him up and ask for a second chance. You used to tell him that I was a good-for-nothing sonuvabitch and wasn't anything compared to him. I heard it.

You didn't hear anything, she said, and grabbed her purse off her chair. She looked like she was about to take off.

Don't leave, I said.

I'm gonna walk the fuck out of here, she said. I'm gonna walk the fuck out of here and get in the car and leave. I'm gonna leave your drunk ass in the middle of nowhere.

It felt like it was getting hotter in there and I could feel the boys at the bar looking over to see what the commotion was. Lisa got loud and teardrops started rolling down her face.

You call out of the blue and ask for a ride, she said. You have the nerve to do that after what you did to that poor little dog? You have the balls to act like it isn't a big deal?

I said I was sorry, I said. That next day. I told you over and over. I said, 'I'm sorry, I'm sorry.'

It doesn't matter, she said, slapping the table. She was heating up like I'd seen her do in the past. There was a point Lisa got to, especially when she was tying one on, where she would get so out of hand there wasn't anything you could do. She didn't care if you were in a bar or a movie or eating dinner somewhere, she'd really lay on the theatrics and put on a hell of a show for everyone within earshot. And that's what she was doing. Getting loud and making a scene. Getting those farmers' attention.

What kind of man does that? she said, ashing her cigarette and knocking back her beer. Throws a poor little dog out the door. I've asked everyone I know. What kind of fucking man does that?

I turned my can of beer around in my hand and tried to keep my head about me. Most of me wanted to get up and really have it out. I wanted to just let years of hurt off my chest and put her right in her place. But I kept saying, Just calm down, okay? I know what I did. I know what I did.

You better know what the hell you did, she said, and put her purse back on the chair. She took another drink and wiped her cheeks dry. I just don't know what the hell goes through your mind sometimes, she said. Half the time I really don't.

I lost my appetite a little after that, but Lisa kept on going with the chicken and the beer. I ordered one more drink and took my time with it. It wasn't about the drinking then, it was about trying to keep everything quiet and sane. I sat there and listened while Lisa went down a mental list of all the things I'd ever fucked up. There were white lies and awful names I'd called her. Things I didn't even remember saying in the first place. She made it abundantly clear that I was a no good piece of shit and had a lot of making up to do.

That red-haired waitress came a couple more times with more food and beer before Lisa laid off. She seemed almost too tired to point her finger at me anymore. She stopped talking and got back to eating and drinking and really focused on that. That's when the door opened. All of us in there, Lisa and me, those fellas at the bar, that red-headed waitress, we all turned to see who it was and a big man walked in. It was dark and hard to make out what he looked like for the sun behind him. He went up to the bartender and asked directions. He said him and his family were pretty turned around and needed to know how to get to Evansville.

After the big man got an answer he stood there for a moment and took the place in like he'd never seen a bar before. He crossed his arms and looked over everything, the stuffed animals and all that. He looked up and down the walls until he came to Lisa and me and then he stared for a good, long time. Lisa asked me what the hell his problem was and I told her I didn't know.

He quit looking eventually and walked over to us. As he got closer my eyes adjusted and I could finally get a good look at him. I could see then that it was Albie. He was covered in sweat and his face was flushed like he'd overheated. Out of his pocket he pulled a handkerchief and patted himself down.

That you, Frank? he said, sidling up to our table.

I froze and my throat got caught. I didn't know what to say. Albie, I said. How're you?

Fine, he said. Good, but we got a little lost out there. Bunch of roads flooded over and I got us running in circles.

That's rough, I said.

You're telling me, he said. I want to get home and I got a tired kid in the back.

I didn't know what else to say, so I said, I hear ya.

Well, he said, looking down at the table and all the empty baskets and cans of beer. I got some directions, so I think I'll hit the bathroom and head on out.

Yeah, I said. You bet.

Albie disappeared into the bathroom for a minute and Lisa asked me who he was. I explained and told her about his getting pulled over and trying to bribe a sheriff and how he'd kicked the habit. Lisa shook her head and sucked on her cigarette. It's not gonna last, she said, exhaling a cloud of gray smoke. She said, Guys like him start sneaking off in the middle of the night and hit up every liquor store in town.

He came back then, Albie did, and he walked outside. Before he did though, he stopped at our table again and put his arm around my shoulder. Frank and me, he said, we go back a couple of months now, and I got to tell you, he was the best guy at the facility. No doubt about it.

Thanks, I said to him. That's awful nice to say.

I mean it, he said. Frank and me are real close.

When he finished saying that he patted me on the back and took off. Lisa and me were alone again and she seemed upset that he'd come over at all. She said, There's something I don't like about him. She said there were all kinds of things she didn't like about him.

Then she started in on me about the dog again, saying I was horrible and such. She said she didn't know if she could ever trust me, not after how I'd behaved. She said there wasn't any way I was going to be able to say I was sorry enough. It was really going to take some work, she said, and then she said she didn't know if she had the patience or the love to see it through.

But I didn't care. Not right then I didn't. I was remembering standing out there by the river and stacking those sandbags. Me and Albie taking turns lifting them out of the mud and trying to build a wall. I felt like I had something I needed to say to Albie right then. I didn't know what it was, all I knew was that I had to get it out. I probably wasn't going to see him again. Surely there was something I needed to tell him. Something I needed said.

Without a word I left Lisa and walked past the farmers at the bar and out the door. The world came at me in a flash of sun and I had to squint real hard to see anything. I did see Albie's car though. It was idling at the end of the lot, right where the gravel met the road. I could see Albie sitting behind the wheel, a map stretched across the dash. There was his wife beside him, her finger tracing a line from one page to another, their boy slumped down, asleep in the back.

I ran up to Albie's window and he jumped up from the map with a start. He rolled down his window and looked at me. There was Albie, the same fella who'd tried to slip a sheriff a twenty dollar bill, the same fella who'd sweated out there at six and seven in the morning, in the rain, in the muck. There were rings under his eyes from where he hadn't slept, but he looked happy and relieved.

What is it? he said, looking up at me. What is it, Frank?

I thought of a lot of things I could've said. I thought maybe I could talk about all of those card games we'd played and all the times him and me and the fellas bullshitted. I wanted to bring up the food and the TV and the games and the path down by the river, the one we'd worked so hard to save. I wanted to bring all of that up, all of that and more, but I couldn't do it. I couldn't make any words.

We're gonna head home now, Albie said. You take care of yourself, Frank. You go and take real good care of yourself.

He rolled up his window, and as he did I looked from him to his plain wife and then into the backseat at their little sleeping boy. His wife was tired too and it didn't seem like the little boy was ever going to wake up. Albie put the car in drive and coasted out. On either side of him were those big lakes of floodwater, shimmering in the sun.

I stood out there alone and looked at those lakes. They stretched out as far as I could see, from the bank of the road and out into the surrounding forests. Every so often a downed tree poked out of the water, but for the most part it was unbroken and the surface reflected the sky so well you could hardly pick out where one ended and the other began. Tired clouds were speeding past and you could watch them glide in the air and on the water.

There wasn't anywhere I needed to be, so I took my time and looked at water running around those trees and houses, and I looked at the little waves rolling by. I thought about the facility and its path under so many feet of dirty water, and I thought about the fellas, Truck going with Charlie Gillen and Pat just leaving, and I wondered where they ended up. And I thought about Lisa, probably into another cigarette and beer, sitting at that table and cursing my name.

I thought maybe I should go back in there and say I was sorry all over again. Maybe even get down on my knees and tell her, Honey, I hate that I ever hurt you, and hope for the best. Way I figured, she'd take me back after I proved to her I was worth the chance. Sure, she'd still sneak off every now and then and make those phone calls. I knew that. There wasn't a doubt in my mind she'd be all over Mike again the second I fucked anything up.

But I also thought better of it. I had the notion to hoof it from there, just take off without saying another word. I thought about heading in the direction Albie and his blue station wagon went and catching up with him at a gas station or hotel or something. If I did I'd remember what I was going to say and then I'd return the favor and put my arm around him. I'd tell that plain-looking wife of his, tell her Albie Jenkins was one of the best son of a bitches I'd ever come across. I'd tell that son of his too, that black-headed boy. I'd look him deep in those eyes and tell him the truth about his old man and life. I'd tell him about paths and dogs and women in bars hovering over baskets filled with crumples of greased paper.

I'd tell him about it all.

EVERYBODY MUST GIVE SOMETHING BACK FOR SOMETHING THEY GET

The morning after the windstorm Claire took her boy for a walk to see the damage. Up and down the block limbs and pieces of torn siding lay in heaps. People were standing in their yards, looking around helplessly.

Looky there, the boy said, pointing to an uprooted tree. Look at that.

That's a big one, isn't it? she said.

Sure is, he said The boy gripped her hand tighter. What made all that happen? he said.

The tree or the storm? she said.

The boy let go and rubbed the tip of his nose with his palm. The storm, he said. Where do they come from?

Claire led him toward Walnut, the street that ran by the city garage where her husband worked, and tried to remember what she'd learned a long time before in a meteorology class in college. She had only gone for a year before getting pregnant with the boy and dropping out, but she could still remember some random information from time to time.

I think, she said, straining to see if her husband was one of the workers sitting out front of the garage, they happen when two kinds of weather meet in one place.

What kind of weathers? the boy said.

Well, she said. There's warm weather and there's cold weather.

Hmm, the boy said. He tapped his chin with a finger from his free hand as if he were deep in thought. And then what? he said.

They fight, Claire said. That's why it gets so scary whenever there's a storm.

The boy accepted it and pulled Claire toward a yard filled with debris. An old, dead tree had split toward the top and fallen into the front porch of a home. The house had glass panels and they had exploded out as if rocked by a bomb. Watering cans, lanterns, ashtrays, brooms, and bags of seed were strewn all the way out to the road.

The boy kneeled down in the mess. He picked up a ceramic bird painted like a cardinal and looked it over. Its beak was broken. Can I keep it? he said, looking to his mother.

The street was empty enough and she looked to make sure no one was watching them. Give it to me, she said, and stuffed it into her purse.

———

For dinner she made some pigs in a blanket and a pan full of fries. Before she pulled them out of the oven the phone rang.

You wouldn't believe it, her husband said. All the way from Apple to College the power's off and the company's saying it'll be two days 'til it's back.

God, she said. It's bad out there.

No shit, he said. We got another couple of hours 'fore we can even think of clocking out.

So Claire and the boy ate dinner alone and talked about his day at school, and when they finished she cleared the plates and took the boy upstairs to get his bath ready. She turned the water on and tested it to make sure it wasn't too hot or too cold. After it was just right she went to clean the dishes. She filled the sink with water and squirted in some soap. By the time she got her hands wet the phone was ringing again.

It was her ex-husband. Claire, he said, don't hang up. Sorry to call. I'm real sorry.

She turned and made sure she was alone before she said anything. Something made her nervous. Her body shook a little and made it hard to speak.

You should be sorry, she said. You can't call here, Sam.

I know, he said. I know, but I'm in a bad place and need-ed someone. He paused for a moment. Someone familiar, he said.

Claire had thoughts of hanging up and unplugging the cord. She thought she might undo all the phones and call to change the number the next day. The Sam she had known was a boozer from way back and he'd been in trouble a few times. In the past she'd answered these calls and found herself rushing out to get a bail bond at 3:30 in the morning or picking him up out on some dirt road where he'd wrapped his truck around a tree.

What is it this time? she said. You need money?

No, he said, and coughed. Nothing like that, he said. There was a moment when she thought maybe the line had gone dead, but he coughed again and went on. Things've been good that way, he said. Got a gig at the lumber yard in Spencer. Pay's not bad.

Claire peered out the blinds to see if her husband had pulled into the carport. I got things to do, she said. I gotta get off here in a short, so cut the chat and get to it.

Sam laughed until it sent him into another fit. Jesus, Vicki, he said. Yes, ma'am.

Vicki was Claire's mother's name and whenever Sam wanted to get her goat he'd call her that. It was something that'd caused more than a handful of fights in the four years they were married.

I'm telling you, Claire said, I don't have time for this shit.

Sure, Sam said. Sorry, I'm just all out of sorts. Y'know? I mean, it's not so bad, us talking. Right?

Claire heard the water shut off upstairs and the boy running to his room. It is what it is, she said.

All right, Sam said. I just wanted to talk. It's been a rough couple of months.

You been drinking? she said.

Now? he said.

Dumb question, she said. Of course you've been drinking. You never stopped.

Another cough. You got me, he said. You really got me.

The boy ran into the kitchen then with his towel draped over his shoulders like a cape. He was wearing underwear and flexing his arms like a bodybuilder.

Go upstairs, Claire said. Get your pajamas on and your book picked out.

Who was that? Sam said.

But Mom, the boy said.

Now, Claire yelled, and the boy dropped the towel and sprinted upstairs. Sorry, she said into the phone.

Was that him? Sam said.

We're not going to talk about him, she said, twisting a knot into the phone cord. Say what you have to say and be done.

Sure, he said. Been a tough little time, y'know? It's just damn good to hear your voice. There was silence. His too, he said.

You got a minute, then I'm hanging up, she said.

Fine, I get it, I do. You have a right to be pissed, I won't deny it. I've done some shit, no doubt. Shit I ain't proud of.

C'mon, she said.

I got lonely, he said. That's all. Was sitting around without lights tonight and got all blubbery. You know how it goes.

Power's out? she said.

Yes ma'am, he said. Got a fridge spoiling in the other room. 'Bout three pounds of pork chops going bad.

Claire opened her ice box and had a look. The light came on and the cold air brushed against her face.

Damn storm was something, wasn't it? he said. Ripped my uncle's garage all to hell.

We had some limbs, Claire said. Nothing too bad.

Yeah, he said. Good. Glad to hear it.

The line filled with static and she could hear something being said, but couldn't make it out. It flooded through until it weakened and died away.

—and that's why I called, he said. The whole thing got me thinking about that storm we had after we moved into our old place.

Another bout of shaking ran through Claire. She hadn't thought of their old place in years. It was a duplex on the west end of town, a brick house split in two with matching concrete patios. Sam and her had celebrated by grilling out there and the sky had gotten darker and darker in the distance. Claire remembered Sam pointing at the clouds with a spatula and saying storms were good omens.

Pretty soon the dusk sky was black and knuckle-sized hail was falling. Not knowing any better, they'd run out into the street to collect big handfuls of ice and had carried it inside. By the time they put it in the freezer the wind and rain had whipped through and swept all their plants and chairs off the patio.

I almost forgot about that, Claire said. Shit, that was bad.

You ain't kidding, Sam said with a laugh. Dented the hell out of the car and wiped out half of town.

Shit, Claire said, unable to say much else.

You remember, he said, going out afterwards and seeing how bad Main Street was?

Trees everywhere, she said. Big ones, too. Pulled right up out of the ground. Fences and the like just everywhere.

You got it, Sam said. And you were going on and on about warm fronts and cold fronts. I think you were in a class then. Weather 101 or something like that.

That's right, she said.

You remember that shop? he said. Down by the theater?

Which one? she said.

The one, he said. Sold all the wigs and costumes?

Okay, she said. I think. Maybe.

Oh, c'mon, he said. It was wrecked. Roof caved in and all kinds of shit lying out in the street?

Maybe, she said, looking out toward the carport again.

You know it, he said. You gotta remember that place. We walked up there and saw all the shit on the sidewalk. The wigs and the clown suit, and you thought it was just the funniest goddamn thing you'd ever seen.

Okay, she said, I dunno.

I found that necklace, he said. The one with the fake diamond on it. With the fake gold chain and the big, fake diamond on it. I had you try it on. Remember?

Claire sighed. Maybe, she said. Long time ago, y'know? Memories get hazy.

Oh, he said. That's too bad. I said you looked like Elizabeth Taylor and we...

 He drifted off and said nothing for a few seconds. Looky there, he said, in shock. Goddamn lights just came back on.

Hearing that made Claire run to the window to check again. Next door, Bill, who also worked for the city, had just pulled in. All right, Claire said. I got to get off here. Nice catching up, but you can't call anymore. Got it?

No, Sam said. I mean, no I won't anymore. Good catching up. You got it.

Okay, she said, still staring out the window.

Okay, he said.

Claire hung up the phone and went upstairs to check on the boy. He was already passed out with half his body falling off the bed. Claire grabbed his legs and moved them gently over and covered him. She went to the bedroom she shared with her husband and changed into a nightgown and got into bed. For a while she read with the light on and waited for him to come home, but that only made her nervous.

After fighting the urge a little while, she went to get her cigarettes from her purse in the kitchen. When she reached in to grab her pack she felt something hard in there and pulled out the cardinal the boy had found. She studied it by the light over the sink and traced her fingers over the rough surface. She felt its broken beak.

She carried the bird upstairs with her cigarettes and got back in bed. Her husband hated when she smoked there. She lit one and took a long, careful draw. She sat the cardinal on a night-stand next to the bed and looked at it from all the different angles.

When she was finished she turned off the light and tried to sleep. She couldn't help but stare at the numbers on the bedside clock. They kept rolling by. She thought about calling the garage, but she knew no one would pick up anyway.

Around two she started picturing him coming in and throwing his wallet and keys on the night stand. He did it every night and Claire got to worrying he would knock that cardinal off and break it. Something about that really bothered her. She thought about it so much it kept her from resting. So she sat up, turned on the light, and carried it over to her dresser.

On top of her dresser was a jewelry box made out of polished cherry wood. Her grandfather had made it for her grandmother and it'd been passed down to her. She opened it and leafed through some drawings the boy had drawn for her. They were of dogs and moons and all the other things boys liked to draw. Under them were letters her husband had written when they first started seeing each other. She looked through them and read a few lines here and there. They were in terrible handwriting and filled with misspelled words, but they were sweet all the same.

She found a spot underneath and placed the cardinal there carefully. The lid wouldn't close just right though with the cardinal standing up, so she reached back in and laid it on its side. Next to it was a small gift box. She took it out and turned it over a few times. Inside was a cheap golden chain. It fell into her hand. The clasp was broken and the gold plating was flecking off. She carried it to bed and raised it up to the light. There was a big glass jewel at the end and it glittered terribly when she held it just the right way.

I BELONG TO YOU,
ALWAYS

Marla left work and stopped by the bakery on her way home.
It was a little shop where bitter old women hunched over
the cases and routinely shortchanged their customers, but they
were the only bakers in town and Marla knew her husband Simon loved their bread more than just about anything.

Sourdough, Marla said to the wilted woman at the register.
One loaf, sliced thin please.

The woman disappeared into the back and left Marla
alone to peruse a display of wedding cakes and freshly made
pies. They were almost perfect, with delicately curled ribbons of
frosting and soft brown crusts. Each looked as if a lifetime had
been spent preparing it.

The woman behind the counter returned empty-handed
and said it would be another ten minutes.

Ten minutes? Marla said.

Three loaves in the oven, the woman said.

Marla looked at the clock on the wall above a table full of

tarts. It was six-thirty already, later than usual for her, but it was Wednesday and she knew Simon liked to take a long walk around the neighborhood on Wednesday and she'd probably have more than enough time to get the bread and fix some kind of dinner before he waltzed in with sweat darkening his shirt and wetting his hair.

While she waited she surveyed the cases some more. Under the lights the frosting shimmered like new snow. There were cakes with words written across their tops like Congratulations, Jim and Marge, and Together Forever. Some even had miniature brides and grooms. One cake was covered in an entire wedding party and a group of onlookers. There was even a preacher standing in front of the happy couple, the good book in his tiny wax hands.

When the bread was brought out it was wrapped in plain white paper and tied off with a piece of string. The woman handed it to Marla and she felt how warm it was. She gave the woman a ten and knew full well not to expect the right amount back.

By the time she returned to her car a sprinkle had come on. The parking lot was spotted dark and the windshield speckled with rain. The air smelled like wet cardboard soaked to the point of collapse. She got in, frustrated that Simon was probably stuck at home and unable to go on his usual Wednesday stroll, and her worry only worsened when she turned her key in the ignition and the sprinkle grew into a downpour.

On the drive Marla drummed the steering wheel and mentally prepared to cook dinner. In her mind she opened the kitchen pantry and looked over what was available. She had looked there enough times that she knew, without a doubt, what she would find. There were some cans of soup and boxes of rice and pasta. Some flour and a bag of beans. But she remembered that she had a carton full of eggs in the fridge and a fresh package of hot sausage in the meat drawer. She remembered how Simon loved it when she fried that sausage up in a skillet with sliced potatoes and onions and cracked an egg over the top so he could spread some butter on his bread and sop up the runny yolk, and her mind was made.

She pulled up in front of the house and saw the lights were off, which was odd because Simon hated a dark home and refused to turn off all the lamps, even before he left for a trip or on one of his walks. She looked at the house and rolled it over in her head for a second before tossing it out and focusing on running through the rain and to the door.

She sopped inside and flipped on all the lights in the living room. She half-expected to find Simon asleep on the couch, the newspaper folded over his chest, as he was wont to do. But there was no Simon. No newspaper.

She checked upstairs. In the bathroom. In the basement. His study, where he sometimes sat with headphones on that cancelled out her calls. But he was nowhere.

It was then that she panicked. Just the week before she'd been watching a news show about a woman who'd worked as a spy for Russia for twenty years. Her husband and kids and neighbors had no idea and then, one day, she was gone, on a jet heading back to her homeland. It happens all the time, she thought as she went to check his closet. People pack up all their things and take off. Never to be seen again.

But his closet was full. Not a shirt or pair of shoes gone. All of his ties in place. Even his hidden stash of money, in a shoebox in the far corner, lay untouched.

She scolded herself for even thinking Simon might step out on her. She'd known him for a dozen years, had been married to him for ten of those, and was certain he could never betray her like that.

He must be walking, she said to herself, making her way to the kitchen. He must've went ahead and gone for one of his walks. Weather be damned.

So she convinced herself and got to work on dinner. She chopped some onions, sliced two potatoes, and threw them into a skillet. They cooked and then she tossed in the sausage alongside them. Before she cracked the egg, she buttered slices of the bread and laid them out with a plate and a cold beer so they'd be ready in case Simon walked in the door with an appetite.

He didn't come home though and the storm grew. The sky lit up with lightning and thunder boomed through the neighborhood. Marla cooked her dinner and grew sick with worry. She could see Simon out there, stuck in the storm, alone, soaked through and lost in the rain. She could almost see him huddled up in some ditch, his teeth chattering and his ears full of the crashing.

It got to be so bad she couldn't focus on the meal anymore. She turned off the stove and grabbed a raincoat out of the closet. She was going to get in her car and find Simon, wherever he was. She was sure he needed her, that he needed her to save him.

On her way out she grabbed her keys off the counter and wrote a quick note in case he came in while she was searching. She had just signed the note Yours, Marla, when she heard a car door close and the sound of wet footsteps squishing towards the front door.

Marla moved so fast toward the front room that she nearly slipped on the kitchen's tile floor. When she opened the door, expecting to find Simon, fully drenched and no doubt shaking and terrified, she was surprised to see a very tall man in a black suit and hat. Water rolled off his shoulders and drizzled off his hat's wide brim.

Marla, puzzled, could only say, You're not Simon.

The man reached to take off his hat and, in the same motion, shrugged off his coat. He dropped them in a wet pile on the floor and motioned to the couch. The man had a bald, glowing head and a pale complexion. Won't you please sit down? he said.

Marla felt as if she had no choice. Her mind raced with a dozen complaints, the quick urgency to call the police, but she went weak and could do nothing but drag herself over to the couch.

The two of them sat across from one another—Marla on the couch and the man in the recliner where Simon sat every night to drink beer and watch baseball. The man clasped his hands and leaned forward. There was something about him, Marla thought, but she couldn't place it.

I'm a friend of Simon's, the man said. My name is Ray.

Oh, Marla said. I'm sorry. I don't think he's ever mentioned you.

No, Ray said. I can't imagine he ever would have. He pulled a handkerchief from his pocket and Marla saw it had RLM monogrammed on it. I'm an old friend of Simon's. Old, old.

Okay, Marla said. She tried to relax and watched Ray dab his face with the handkerchief. He was a strange-looking man with a very long head and a weak chin below his thin, colorless lips. He looked tired and very odd.

I don't know quite how to say this, Ray said. I've been thinking all day about how I was going to say this.

Marla said okay again, because there was nothing else she could think to say. She wanted to hop right up and bolt for the door, throw it open and rush out into the storm, but she couldn't make herself move for anything.

What I'm going to tell you, Ray said, you're not going to believe. Not at first.

Marla felt herself go rigid. Are you an attorney? she said. Are you Simon's attorney?

Ray laughed. At first he chuckled and waved the handkerchief as if it were a flag, but then the laughter caught on in a very unnatural, forced kind of way, and his whole body moved as if it was out of his control.

No, he said. My goodness, no ma'am.

There was a silence between them and Ray dabbed at his face again. Marla noticed then that the soft folds over his eyes were hairless, and that he was hairless altogether, and she squinted a bit and thought he looked, in that moment, like a great, pale worm.

What you have to understand, he said, is that Simon's time was up. He had to go.

Go? Marla said. Go where? Is he all right? Tell me he's all right.

He's fine, Ray said. Perfectly fine. I saw him this afternoon and he couldn't be better. Fit and healthy. Fit as a, a... Ray seemed to search for a second before saying A fiddle?

Marla nodded. She rocked a bit and could feel the room warming.

Simon is a very brave man, Ray said, patting his temples with the handkerchief. What he did was so very brave.

As she listened, Marla waited for the door to open. She sat there, a sweat building on her, and waited for Simon to burst in and find her sitting there with this man. He would toss Ray out, she thought. Toss him right out into the wet street.

What you have to understand, Ray said, is how important his work was. Just how vital it was to our cause.

Sweat dripped down Marla's face. It felt like the heat was coming off Ray, like it was rolling off him in waves.

We've come so far, Ray said. We've come so far just by studying his work. The data is just astounding.

Where is he? Marla said.

No, no, no, Ray said, shaking his bald head. Not where, dear child. When. *When.*

The room spun for Marla and she clutched the arm of the couch.

We're not so lucky, Ray said. We don't have these, what you call, feelings, where I'm from. Where we're from. We don't have these wild emotions.

Ray laid his handkerchief across his knee and reached into another one of his pockets. From there he pulled a long, thin cigarette and a metal lighter. He bit the cigarette between his white teeth and lit it. He took a healthy puff and exhaled a blue stream of smoke.

We've been reading his numbers, he said. This whole time. Forty years' worth of data. Childhood birthday parties, athletic conquests, broken hearts. Unabashed, soul-crushing loneliness.

He pulled the cigarette from his mouth and studied it with a smile.

But none of it compares to the data he gained from you, Marla.

She yelled for him. Simon! Simon! But he didn't come.

Oh, Ray said, how rich your love was. How kind you were. Selfless. And how beautiful it was, poring over those hours and hours of surveillance of the two of you making love. Groaning and sweating. He took another drag off his cigarette. Telling him, Simon, I am yours. Forever. I belong to you, always.

Ray leaned back and let loose another cloud of smoke that reached for the ceiling.

I taught a course last spring on your trip to Maine, he said. Lectured to auditoriums full of our best and brightest about how you swept the hair from his face while you laid in bed, listening to the ships in the bay. Brilliant.

You have to understand, he said, leaning forward, urgency seeping into his voice. We lost that along the way. We built great cities. We perfected the species. But we lost something. He ashed his cigarette onto the floor and lowered his voice. But you helped us find *it*, he said. You helped us all.

Ray stood up again and seemed so much taller than he had before. Even now, he said, Simon is in a laboratory, recounting the times he's enjoyed with you, telling hundreds of our best scientists all your shared moments and secrets. And they're scribbling furiously on their clipboards and crunching the numbers. We are all so very eager.

Marla watched him stride unnaturally to the wet pile of clothes by the door. He picked up his hat and slipped his coat on. He reached for the door and looked back toward Marla.

Thank you, he said. You haven't even the slightest idea of the good you've done.

And then, like that, he was gone, slunk back into the night, back into the storm. Marla was left there, on the couch, her eyes welled up but unable to cry. The heat had gone too, sure, but she was left to wait for the door to open again. For Simon to bound in and tell her it was all right and not to worry. Not to even pay that man a piece of mind. But she was left to wait, all the same, and what an awful long wait that would be.

LOOSE HIM
AND LET HIM GO

My papa was the biggest man I'd ever seen. His shoulders were broad, his feet were as wide as dresser drawers, and his hands were the size of catcher's mitts. He spoke softly. There were days he must've drank cases of beer, but I never saw him drunk. To think of him now is to think of a mountain that drifted from room to room.

When I remember him, when I really sit down at night and peel away the time, I see him as he was back in the summer of my tenth year, sitting on my momma's back step and pinching a Lucky between his thick fingers. His white hair blowing in the breeze and sweat starting to bleed through his undershirt. At his side was Old John, a crippled beagle that followed Papa most everywhere.

I asked Papa what was wrong with Old John.

He said, He ain't long for this world. Got stiffness in the back legs so bad they drag. Your memaw won't let me put him down.

The idea of Old John dying made me sad as hell back in the day. Sure, he cried most of the time and he had sores that smelled of death, but to look into those big milky eyes of his was to see sympathy living and breathing.

I thought, then at least, that maybe Papa was just tired. The cousins were in town and patience was in low supply for everybody.

You see that? my papa asked, pointing down to the pond. My cousin Jeremiah and my cousin Joseph were smacking the fish they'd caught that day with one of my daddy's hammers. That right there is a shame. Those boys don't give two shits 'bout nothing. Now you know better, don't ya? I nodded and Papa took a swig of his beer. Not a one of your cousins gonna amount to a thing. Not a one of 'em.

Just then my momma poked her head out the screen door. Daddy, she said. You reckon you and Jacob can run into town and get some things?

With a groan my papa stood and hitched up his slacks. I remember being so excited to run into town with him because that was just about the biggest honor in the whole world. His truck was spotless and there were big firebirds stitched into the seat cushions, and whenever Papa drove he listened to his country radio as loud as it would go. He'd sing along in a voice so perfect you swore he was better than any of those fake old cowboys the disc jockeys played.

I said, Papa, are you a cowboy?

He spit out the window. Hell no. Cowboyin's rotten work. Shovelin' shit all day and sleeping with a rock in your back. Fuck no, I ain't no cowboy.

I kept quiet the rest of the way and watched him drive. The wheel seemed tiny in his hands and his head looked like it might bust through the roof if we hit a big enough bump in the road. Old John was between us and having a really hard time breathing.

We got to Goodman's Store and left Old John in the truck while we went inside. The place had four aisles and a cooler with packages of meats and cheeses. The last aisle, over by the tackle boxes, was full of candies and gum. I was going over there when Papa grabbed my arm and told me not to stray too far.

After he went in the back with Mr. Goodman, I made my way over to the candy. Daddy and Momma had always been poor and I never got many treats, so it all looked mighty fine in those packages. There was licorice and lemon drops and chocolate peanuts and just about every kind of candy you'd ever hope to see. I was so busy inspecting the spice drops I didn't even hear the bell above the door jingle.

I was just fine, there with the candy and such, that is, until a man sidled up to me and tapped me on the shoulder. Now, I don't scare easy, even when I was just a boy, but this man was unsettling from the get-go. He was bald and his face was covered in big purple blotches that ran from his brow to his cheeks. He had no teeth and his breath smelled like Old John's sores.

He said, You're Noah Brown's grandbaby, ain't ya?

I am, I said.

I can tell, he said. You got the Brown look to ya. Gonna be a big man someday. Say, my name's Ed Owings. Your granddaddy ever make mention of me?

I tried to remember a time, but couldn't. Something about the guy was making me nervous, so I tried to walk away but he pulled me back.

He said, Let me show you something, and held out the palm of his right hand. There was a smudge there as black as a storm cloud. You know what that is?

I told him I didn't.

That right there, he said, is the point in which God's judgment entered me.

Papa still wasn't there.

Back in those days I drank and cavorted, Ed said. I was walking home from the bar one night and the sky opened. I ask you, son, do you know what it's like to be struck by lightning?

I said no.

Imagine, he said, tossing his hands about. Imagine the living, burning embrace of Jehovah entering through the palm of your hand and running through every part of your body at the temperature of the sun.

I told him I didn't want to.

No one does, he said with a chuckle. Say, he said, getting serious. You want to know what happens when you die?

I was going to say no but he didn't give me the chance.

You're led into a room with three baskets, he said. You get to look inside and choose one.

Again, I looked for Papa.

Each basket holds life and death and suffering, he said and laughed. And I was about to pick when your granddaddy pulled me back. He said, Ed, you ain't ready yet. Christ, ain't that something?

I said sure and pulled away. Wasn't anyone else in that store save for the two of us and I was starting to get real scared so I yelled out, yelled with every bit of strength my little body had.

There ain't no need to yell, Ed said. I just want your grand-daddy to send me back, that's all.

Right then Papa whipped around the corner with a sack of groceries under each arm. When he saw Ed there his eyes narrowed and the cigarette fell from his lips.

Noah, Ed cried. Thank God you're here. Oh, Noah, the pain's *so* bad—

My papa dropped those sacks and pulled me away by the arm. There was fear in his face. We walked out and Ed was still in the aisle just a-sobbing. I've never seen my Papa like that in my whole life. Not once.

I said nothing the whole ride home and Papa never turned on the radio. The only sound in the truck was Old John wheezing and carrying on. With each breath came the sorriest cry you're ever likely to hear. It went on and on until I had to put my hands over my ears and pray it would go away.

It got so bad Papa pulled over alongside the road. He stroked what was left of Old John's fur and said, I reckon you've been about the best friend an old man like me could have ever had.

Then Papa held out one finger, a long tobacco-stained finger, and touched the valley between Old John's cataract-filled eyes. The struggle was over. That dog was gone. Just as silent and calm as those fish Jeremiah and Joseph were beating on the pond's sandy shore.

When we got home Papa carried Old John down into the woods in the crook of his arm and found a spot between two elm trees to lay him to rest. After patting down the dirt and wiping the sweat from his brow, Papa turned back to the house. I stayed there awhile, watching the way the wind played with the soil and the leaves in the trees. My cousins were off a ways, firing their twenty-two's at squirrels or starlings or whatever living thing crossed their paths, but I just sat there 'til the day bled into night, wondering, when my time came, when choosing came to choosing, which of the baskets would be mine to keep.

THE NORTH END
OF TOWN

There's this fella been hanging around. Older guy with gray hair and a little thin mustache. Dresses in jeans and a dirty sweatshirt and wears a pair of tennis shoes that are just about ready to fall apart. Seems like I see him every day. At the bar, the shops, the stores. I see him in the street so much he's starting to nod whenever we pass. No big deal. I got a ton of people I don't know saying hello. That's not the problem. It's that he always carries around this yellow umbrella and he's got it opened all the time.

Couple of weeks ago I was having lunch with my sis at this Mexican place on the corner. We were sitting in a booth by the window and were finished eating at that point. We were just sitting there watching the people walk by. Every once in a while Sis would start talking about how she was having a hard time with her husband. Said he seemed like a different person. Like he'd given in to bad intentions and savagery.

Sometimes, she said, I think he wants to kill me. Like he'd rather kill me than spend another second with me.

Huh, I said.

It's bad, she said. He doesn't even want to come to bed with me. I try and stay up and wait for him to get tired, but he never does. Finally I gotta just turn in. And he's up watching TV or doing whatever it is he does the rest of the night. The whole thing's just awful.

Just then the guy walked past. It was seventy degrees, not a cloud in the sky, and

sure enough he still had that umbrella open. I about lost it then.

Do you see that? I said to my sis. Doesn't matter what it's like outside, he's always got his umbrella open. I'm telling you, it could be the nicest day you ever saw and he'd have that thing out.

Maybe he likes it, my sis said.

Likes it? I said. What's to like about a crummy old umbrella? Really, what's to like about an umbrella?

Another time I was at the store and here he comes. Sure enough, he had that thing open. Imagine that. That takes some kind of nerve if you ask me, walking around a store with an open umbrella. And he looked just as happy as could be, strolling down the aisle with his umbrella out for all to see.

It got so bad for me I couldn't sleep. I'd lie down and try to go under but couldn't keep my mind from racing. I kept thinking about him and that umbrella. It was so clear to me that I could picture it, you know? Like it'd been burned into my brain. I'd go to work and have a ton of stuff to get done and all I could do was sit there and get pissed off about some prick and his yellow umbrella.

I'd had enough and knew I had to say something. It got to the point either I was going to or lose my ever-loving mind. So

I waited until I saw him again. I had it all planned out. I was going to go up to him and ask him what the deal was with the umbrella. Very simple-like. Hey, I'd say, what's up with you and the umbrella? Not a big deal at all, just a concerned citizen seeking answers.

But then I didn't see him. I didn't think it was a big deal when the first or second day went by, but by the time the third rolled around I was starting to get nervous. What if I never saw him again? What if he'd left the neighborhood for good? Then I'd have to walk around for the rest of my life wondering just what the hell was with that umbrella. A week rolled by and then another. Sometimes I'd think I'd see him coming into a shop or a restaurant and I'd get real excited, like it was Christmas all over again. But it wasn't him. It was always some other old guy who had the courtesy to close his umbrella when he came inside.

Pretty soon I asked around and my buddy down at the doughnut shop didn't know him and the bartender at Jessie's said he'd seen him around before but couldn't remember how long it'd been. I was stopping people on the street and asking. People who didn't know me from Adam. You know this umbrella guy? I'd say, and they'd give me a look like I was crazy. I went down to the churches and checked around. The post office. I even went to the food bank and the pawn shop. No one had a clue who this guy was.

I'd given up on ever seeing him again and I was in a real bad place for it. I started drinking all hours of the day. Almost lost my job before the boss sat me down and let me know how close I was to being let go. Get a grip on yourself, he said. Get some fresh air. Get some sleep.

So I took a week off and ended up sitting around my apartment the whole time, watching for any sign of the guy. I never wanted to leave my window. I stayed there all day and watched. Getting up for a drink or to take a shower was awful because I was so nervous I'd miss him I'd get the shakes and start sweating like crazy. I couldn't even butter a piece of bread I was shaking so bad. I knew it would be just my luck for him to walk by when I wasn't looking.

A couple of weeks later I saw him. It was the best thing I'd seen in a long time. He was taking a turn at the corner and was coming down my sidewalk. I knew because I saw that umbrella. I knew as soon as I saw it. I jumped up from my chair and hauled ass out the door and down the stairs. He'd gone past my front door when I got out there and I had to run a little to catch up.

I was about to tap him on the shoulder to get his attention when there came an awful noise from down the street. A blue Plymouth had slid through a light and slammed into the passenger side of a brown Ford. When it hit there was a crunch loud enough that everyone around turned and looked, and the guy with the umbrella and me weren't any different. We were both standing there looking at the wreck.

The guy driving the Ford was the first one to get out of his car. He jumped out and started cussing the other guy out right off. He was calling him a sonuvabitch and all kinds of things by the time the guy got out of his Plymouth. The Plymouth guy was messed up and shaking his head. He looked sorry as hell, really. You could tell he was saying it too. The Ford guy wasn't about to lay off though. He kept yelling and was getting right up in his face. From as far away as we were you could see the spit flying from his mouth.

It seemed like the whole thing went on forever, the Ford guy yelling at the Plymouth guy. Jabbing his finger into his chest and pointing back to his car. Then the Ford guy swung and landed a shot right on the chin that knocked down the Plymouth guy. Landed on the ground and didn't get back up. The Ford guy started kicking him in the side and the head.

While that deal was going down I'd forgotten about the guy with the umbrella. Had nearly forgotten all about it until he said something. It was something like Oh my God or something just like it. I heard him say that and it reminded me. I mean, I turned back to him and saw that dumb umbrella and I was mad all over again. I grabbed his shirt and slammed him up against the side of a building. Pushed him against the brick and got right up in his face.

Why? I said. Why the fucking umbrella, huh? I think that's what I said. I know I got it out at some point. Everything was running together at first and I was talking crazy. Words that didn't mean anything. Gibberish, I guess. But I got it together eventually. I was asking why the hell anyone would keep his umbrella open all the time. Why the hell it was so goddamn important to have a goddamn umbrella when it was sunny and nice out. Why was it so important?

He didn't say anything at first. He just looked at me with these real surprised eyes and held that umbrella to his chest like it meant his life. That little mustache of his started bobbing up and down. At one point he cried a little and it made me so angry I slapped him across the face. It drew some blood from his nose. I kept asking him why he kept his umbrella like that, why he needed to show it off to anyone and everyone. Then he started full-on sobbing and saying nonsense things. He wasn't saying anything about the umbrella or anything I cared about so I kept shaking him and pushing him against the wall. But no matter how hard I shook him he wouldn't tell me what I wanted to know. He just wouldn't. I had to let him go and he ran off. He dropped his umbrella on the sidewalk and ran off just as fast as he could.

I don't see him anymore. Guess he went and got himself a moving van and headed for the suburbs. Guess I can't blame him anyway. Read in the news today that the guy driving the Ford kicked that other guy so hard he had a stroke. Broke a couple of ribs and put some fluid on his brain. There was a big write-up that said he might never talk again. Nobody has to tell me anything. It's getting rough out there.

TO THE THIRSTY
I WILL GIVE

Cable TV was the first thing to go when times got rough for Billy and June. They'd had a hell of a fight, what with June claiming she couldn't go without her Food Network and Billy promising they'd re-up as soon as his buddy Leroux got his boat fixed and the checks came rolling in. Of course, Katrina had all but totaled the Fickle Lady and repairs were slow in the making. Then, as soon as they'd got her back in shape and out on the water, the goddamn BP well spilled and fucked everything up again. After that they'd had to buy the cheap groceries at Rouse's and sleep with the windows open in lieu of the state-of-the-art AC unit Billy'd put in the summer before.

But the loss of programming haunted them. When Billy wasn't working he'd park himself on the couch and watch whatever the hell came across the local channels. June got tired of all the shows on there and would pace until she couldn't stand it anymore and had to leave. In the afternoons Billy didn't mind that so much. There were only a few places she could go really.

Down to Sammy's to get a po' boy or maybe to the waterfront to watch the Gulf roll in. There wasn't much trouble to get into either way, and after she'd gone Bobby could make himself a sandwich in peace and grab a couple of cold ones out of the icebox. Concentrate on daytime soaps with a clear head about him.

The evening was a different story. She was always going in the other room and making secret phone calls. Putting on her best dresses and shaving her legs. He knew she had someone on the side. A businessman out of Houston named Walter who liked to call her pussycat and asked if she was going to be a dirty girl for him. Billy had read the e-mails and everything. Whenever June got in the shower he snuck her computer out of its case and logged on. He listened for the water to get going and went through all their messages.

The things he read were pretty typical for the most part, but grew exceptionally raunchy in places. The one that got him the best was when the businessman had written to June early on that he couldn't stop thinking about the way she tasted and that he was starving for her. Attached to the bottom of the e-mail was a picture. The first time Billy opened it up he couldn't believe it. The businessman looked old and boring, a gap between his huge white teeth. When Billy was working, wrenching in those nets on the Fickle Lady, he could put that picture out of mind for a while, but with the ship and her crew grounded he had all the time in the world to sit and stew over it.

That morning he had the businessman on his mind while he watched a show where rich people led cameras through their houses and showed off their custom pools and wall-sized stereo systems. The guy on that episode was telling the cameraman to get a real good shot of the life-sized marble statue of himself he kept in his living room. Billy didn't know what to think of that. He was too busy imagining that businessman laying June across a bed and eating her from the feet up like a big ol' steak. In his mind he was picturing him finishing her and smacking his lips like he'd just eaten the finest piece of meat ever. That's when June came in the living room and asked for the keys to the car. She smelled like perfume and had her hair done something beautiful.

I need the Honda, she said.

Normally Billy would've just handed her the keys. He knew she liked to head over to her sister's and drink wine and complain about him, but he got the feeling that wasn't the plan. The e-mails had started up again and he knew the businessman was going to be in town and wanted to see her.

Reckon you're gonna meet up with Walter tonight, Billy said.

June plopped down on the chair next to the couch and pulled a tube of lip gloss out of her oversized purse. Who the fuck is Walter? she said, unfazed and rolling the gloss carefully over her mouth. You're all the time going on about Walter. I don't know nobody named Walter.

Bet you don't, Billy said. Listen. How about you stay in? Maybe we'll pop some corn and watch a movie or two. Finish off that wine in the fridge and sit out back awhile?

June dropped the tube into her purse. Yeah, she said, But I got plans. I'm meeting Sis down at Harry's. Her and Jeff ain't getting along too good.

Billy nodded. She always had an excuse handy and there wasn't no use arguing. Instead he looked to the TV again where the guy was in swimming trunks now and diving underwater. The camera went down with him and there were big TVs built into the walls of the pool. The water was so clear you could get down there and watch whatever you wanted.

Why you got this shit on? June said. I mean, there ain't no reason to watch shit like this.

Better than news, Billy said, tipping back his drink. Hell, I can't stand to turn it on anymore. You know they got a TV camera down there and you can watch that motherfucking well leak all day long? You can sit right here in your goddamn underwear and watch the goddamn world fall apart.

June rolled her eyes and went into the kitchen to look for the keys to the car. She searched through a stack of overdue bills and around a half-dozen cans lining the counter. Christ, she yelled to Billy. Reckon you might slow down maybe?

Slow down? Billy said. I'm taking it slow.

For a moment June paused. She picked one of the cans off the counter and tossed it into the trash nestled between the range and the icebox. It rattled in and she soon followed it with another and another. You get mean, she said. You know it well as I do. You get to drinking and you turn mean.

Billy mouthed a whatever and finished off his beer. Better get heading, he said to her. Gonna be late for your date with Walter.

He waited for some kind of smart remark or another lie, but all he heard was the door slam.

After a couple of minutes, when he was sure she was gone, he hurried off the couch and found her computer where she hid it under the dresser. He got on there and read through her messages all over again. They were ridiculous notes punctuated by ridiculous looking smiling and winking faces. Some of them had little cartoon hearts at the bottom. He read from the start, read the early ones about how they'd met downtown at The Top Hat and messed around in the businessman's Hyundai. He even read over the two week period the winter before when the businessman had gone real soft and started asking her to run away and marry him. He'd said if she would divorce Billy he'd make her a real honest woman and take care of her. That only lasted for twelve days though, and as soon as she'd entertained it he took the offer back and said he just wanted something to do whenever he came to town.

Billy sat there and reopened the wound. He went through all of those messages, even the ones that hurt him the most. The ones that described in terrible detail what the businessman wanted to do to June and what he'd already done. Billy dragged the computer's cursor over every single pussycat and every single mention of the parts of June that Billy thought she'd kept for him and him alone. He read right up to the latest e-mail, dated five hours earlier. It said the businessman would be setting up at a place called Lucky Lucky, a hip little hangout on the other end of town where all the big shots went to seal deals.

juney, the e-mail read. gonna b around at 9 or so. u should come by and wear one of those dresses u look so good in and nothing under it. u know how i like it lol.

He signed it w.

Right away Billy could picture the whole scene. The two of them sitting in a booth in the corner, a plate of fries and a couple of beers sweating on their table. Aerosmith or some other bullshit rock 'n roll band playing over the stereo while a bunch of fat-faced yes-men patted each other on the back. That businessman running one of his hands through June's pretty done-up hair and sliding the other up the fat of her thigh.

The fucking nerve of it, Billy thought. The goddamned fucking nerve.

He shut down her computer and put it back in the case where she'd left it and pulled on some shoes and a shirt and headed out the door. What he needed was to get a good stiff drink in him and think things out. Part of him wanted to go right down to Lucky Lucky and cause a big goddamn scene. Maybe haul his shotgun with him and put the barrel in that businessman's crawl and see how he liked it. But he knew that was a terrible idea and that he shouldn't run up there with a head full of pissed off. He'd seen too many stories on the news about boys who'd lost their fucking minds and laid waste to a houseful of people.

Billy needed someone to talk it over with, and he knew just who to go to. Two doors down his neighbor Red lived in a double-wide that stretched diagonally across a lot that was lined on all sides by big tiger statues. Some were painted orange and black, bits of red for their maws and white for their long, curved teeth, but some were done up in purple and gold to honor Louisiana State University, Red's son's alma mater. Most of the time Red took up residence in a fold-out chair in the front yard, right next to a weather-beat picnic table Billy had helped drag out of the county dump.

That's where Billy found him, a beer nestled between his legs. He had himself a little command center out there with a pair of black and white TVs sitting on the picnic table in front of him. There were wires and extension cords snaking around his feet and heading back into the trailer.

If it ain't my favorite person, Red said, not even looking up.

Billy grabbed a folding chair for himself out of the dirt and set it up right next to Red, who reached down and fished a beer for Billy out of an ice chest. The can was cold in Billy's hand and he sat there and felt the sweat roll off onto his fingers.

You wouldn't believe this shit, Red said, popping one open for himself and pointing at footage of the well spewing into dark water. They were sayin' just a second ago that they're thinkin' bout dropping a a-tomic bomb down there.

I'll be damned, Billy said.

Seriously, Red said. He settled back in his chair and kicked his feet up onto the picnic table. His sneakers had faded from white to yellow and the soles were starting to come loose and flap around like starving mouths. Up and down his skinny legs were veins that looked to Billy to be some kind of map to a highway system shot to hell. Red said, These motherfuckers are talking about dropping a goddamn a-tomic bomb in the goddamn ocean.

Gulf, said a voice coming out of the trailer. It was Red's third wife, Angela, peeking around the doorway. It ain't an ocean, it's the Gulf of Mexico. She rolled her eyes to Billy. How goes it, honey? she asked.

Billy raised his beer at her and forced his best smile. Makin' it, he said.

She said, Ain't we all, and ducked back inside.

Red matched her rolling eyes with a pair of his own. Y'know that woman won't watch a lick of news? Just flat out refuses to keep up on any of this shit.

I'm the same way, Billy said. Can't hardly stand it.

Red took a slug from his beer and put it in a holder in his chair. That's a mistake, he said, shaking his head. There's big shit comin' to pass right now. Charlie down the street said he heard on the radio that this whole spill thing's a sham. Red paused to look both ways, his eyes narrowing. Said the U-nited Nations has got troops floating off the coast. That this whole thing is just some kind of distraction.

Billy nodded because he didn't know what to say and turned his can of beer around in his hand a couple of times.

These fuckers, Red said. They're just waitin' to take over. Believe you me. They get us good and distracted and they'll be here quicker than shit. Ready to start up their new world order. Don't give one shit about us a 'tall.

For a little while Billy listened to Red rant on about conspiracies and radio programs that only came across the air at two or three in the morning. But then, like most times with Red, Billy tuned him out and focused on things at hand. He thought about June and the businessman, probably a couple of drinks in and getting a little frisky. Maybe the two of them were dancing out on the floor, like tourists did, swaying back and forth and rubbing up on each other.

Trying to distract himself he looked at the TV again. One of the sets was still showing the spill, but the other had moved to an aerial view. The oil was spreading through the water like a bruise. Then it showed some men in ties on a boat. Their sleeves were rolled up to show they'd been doing a hard day's work. They shook their heads and put their hands on their hips.

Red yelled, Do something, before getting himself another beer. The men in ties didn't seem to hear him though. They just stood there with their mouths open, like fish trying to catch flies. Then the footage switched and showed them walking down a beach covered in globs of oil the size of tennis balls. One of the men, an older fella with a buzz cut, squatted down in the sand and scratched his chin. He looked like he was thinking, like he was giving it a good go-over in his head. After a couple of seconds he reached down and touched a single ball of tar with the tip of his finger. He stayed there for a moment before standing up and wiping his hand off on his slacks.

Listen, Red said, after a while. Something we need to talk about, but you're gonna want some grass first.

He reached into his shirt pocket and pulled out a small wooden box. He turned it over in his calloused hands and slid the top open. A little one-hitter popped out and he handed it to Billy, who grabbed a lighter off the picnic table and took a drag. Red sighed and sat up, putting his arms on his knees. He said, We was out the other night, me and Angela, down in the Quarter. We saw June up there.

Billy lit the hitter again and sucked in what was left of the pot. With a fella? he said, spitting out smoke.

Yeah, Red said, leaning back again. There was a fella.

Lemme guess, Billy said. He handed the hitter over and watched Red fix it up again. He said, Older guy. Looked like he might've had some money.

Red ground the hitter into the box and brought it up to his lips. He puffed on it in short little gasps, like he was trying to get a breath. Yes sir, he said. That's the one.

The two of them sat and watched the TVs for a minute or two. They passed the hitter back and forth until there wasn't anything left to smoke. After they'd finished off the beers in the ice chest, Red went inside and reappeared with an arm-full. He bent over with a shallow grunt and dropped them into the ice.

The damndest thing about it, he said, sitting down, was that she saw us too. I mean, me and Angela were sitting a couple tables away and she kept looking over and smiling and waving. Like she couldn't give two shits.

Some people, Billy said.

Some people, Red repeated.

Angela poked her head out again and yelled over to Billy. I'm sorry, honey. We was gonna tell you that night but we didn't know how to go about it. I mean, it's a real goddamn shame.

It is, Billy said.

I mean it, Angela said, before disappearing. Shit don't make sense anymore, she said.

———

Before Billy left Red told him a story. It was about his ex-wife and how she'd stepped out on him. She'd been his first wife, the girl he'd married straight out of high school. The two of them were together for nine long years, Red said, and then she'd gone out of her mind.

Something gets into people, he said. Something gets into 'em and screws up all their circuits. Doesn't matter what you do or what you say, it's too late. You can beg and promise. I mean, I got right down on my goddamn knees and it didn't even phase her. She just dragged me around the kitchen until I let go.

Billy reached down and swatted at a bug that'd landed on his ankle.

Red said, I loved that woman. I mean el-oh-vee-ee-dee. Hell, still do. She could call me up tonight and ask me to up and leave Angela and I probably wouldn't think twice 'bout it. This is serious stuff I'm talking about here.

What I'm trying to say, he continued, is that it ain't your fault. Not that I know of, anyway. Something happens somewhere along the way and everything gets shot all to hell. She was good and faithful to me for nine years and then one day she starts stayin' out all hours of the night. Fucked everybody from here to Shreveport. Boys she met in the frozen food section of the store. Guys we went to school with. Fuck. Even this old prick who was friends with her dad. I'm trying to say it doesn't matter a lick if they got that fucked up wiring.

Billy thought it over. He'd heard people say all of it before. That anybody could wake up one morning and be a different person. He'd seen it with his own dad, who'd packed up his car while Billy's mom was working at the phone company and took off for the West Coast. Told Billy and his little sister Sharon that they probably wouldn't be seeing him anymore and that they should tell their mom thanks for the memories.

He knew it happened. Things change, after all. They go all to hell.

But he'd never figured June to be that way. The two of them had always been solid. They used to talk and make love all hours of the day. Go down to the store and get a six-pack, take it over to The Fly and watch the barges roll down the river. Get good and drunk and fall all over each other in the back of his old Ford. There were good times, a shit-load more than the bad, and the math just didn't figure to him.

Look, Red said, drunk and fighting to stand up. It's dark and I'm hittin' the sack. Been out here all day drinking like there ain't no tomorrow. He staggered to his feet and put the last

of his cans on the picnic table. But I want you to know somethin',
he said. I know how ya feel. When Sharon stepped out on me
I felt like I'd just been beat all to hell. Couldn't hardly get up in
the morning. Couldn't eat. Couldn't do much of anything. But,
he said. I also know there was another side to that coin.

What's that? Billy said.

Well, Red said. I used to take drives back then. Over to
wherever she was shacking up at the time. And most nights she
went to this fella's place. This bastard named Sholes. He was a
teacher over at the community college and was too good for us
piss-ants. Liked to talk down to us after he got a couple of gin
and tonics in him.

Red grabbed a plastic bag from just inside the trailer and
went to work picking up trash. He grabbed each can off the
table and crushed them in his hands. They doubled over like
animals with broken backs. He said, I went over there and just
sat in his driveway. Hell, I could see 'em making it through the
curtains some nights. And I just sat there in my car, drinking
and holding my gun.

When the cans were all cleared he picked up the ice chest
and dumped it onto the ground. The ice melted quickly and left
a dark stain in the dirt. I'm just sayin', he said. I know the other
side of that coin.

———

Half in the bag, Billy went for a walk. He wound through
the neighborhood and past all of his neighbors. They were
in their trailers or houses, their windows glowing in the dark.
Down a ways, past the post office, there were some guys drink-

ing outside a liquor store. As he walked by he could hear them talking about people turning sick. They said with all that oil burning out there on the water they weren't a bit surprised.

He walked further, past his neck of the woods and down to the waterfront. There were bars and restaurants and stores lining the streets, but only a few were open. From what he could see the only people in there were the old timers, the drunks who came out every night to sit and nod their heads to the music on the jukebox. There were a couple of them on the patio of a place Billy liked to go. They were playing chess on a concrete table, but neither one of them seemed to be paying much attention.

Down by the water he found the Fickle Lady in her dock. She bobbed lazily on the water and groaned. She was a good-for-nothing piece of shit boat and, to Billy, it almost seemed like justice that she was grounded. How many times, after all, had she taken on water in the middle of a trip? Almost daily him and the rest of the fellas would have to leave their nets and go below deck to find and plug whatever new hole had sprung up. It was a chore that left them constantly soured and on edge.

He'd gotten so used to the Fickle Lady's problems that some nights, when he lay down to sleep, he had terrible nightmares about her. He dreamed that he was alone at the helm, steering her past the elbow of Florida and into the great, wide Atlantic. And every wave, every great swell of the ocean, loomed over him and the boat and threatened to destroy her and leave him afloat. The water kept coming and coming, filling his lungs with salt and angry foam. It was so vivid, so awful, that he could hear the tearing of her bearings even after he'd snapped awake.

It depressed him to look at that wreck, so he walked further. A mile or two out and he saw lights up ahead. He knew he was getting closer to the road Lucky Lucky was on. All of the walking had put him in a better place and he wanted no part of laying into either June or the businessman at that point. It was hot and a sweat had broken out and covered him, bleeding out his anger. But he still wanted to see them, wanted to go and at least get a good look at the two of them sitting there together and the big goddamn smiles on their faces. So he trudged on, past a couple more neighborhoods and finally to where the tourist part of town started. There were bars with neon lights and booming music leaking out the doors. Big metal fans everywhere pushing mists of cold water at people passing by. Here and there half-dressed girls stood out in the street asking men to come inside and watch them dance. Tourists were sitting on the curbs, drinking and fumbling drunkenly with their bags and purses.

Lucky Lucky sat wedged between a seafood restaurant and another bar called Frisky. The restaurant was closed and a sign hung on the door read, in thick, black letters, Fuck BP. The two bars were in better condition though. People spilled out of them and stood on the sidewalks with oversized cocktails and bottles of beer. Billy pushed his way inside Lucky Lucky and found it packed to the point where he couldn't find a place to stand. Everywhere he moved were folks in fancy clothes, drinking and talking, some dancing to the music while they waited on drinks. Heat fell off the crowd and made the bar swelter to the point that Billy's sweat grew and soaked through his shirt and jeans. It seemed like all of the people were wearing cologne or perfume because it mixed together and created a stink that hung in the air and stung his nose.

Finally he made it to the bar. He fought his way between two older men with ties hanging from their necks in loose knots.

Beads of sweat poured down their temples and into the shoulders of their white dress shirts. They were chain smoking and pointing at one of the TVs hanging over the bar where a baseball game was on. Right next to it, on another set, was the same shot of the well leaking Billy had been watching in Red's front yard.

One of the men started talking about the Rangers when the bartender came around and handed Billy a menu. He opened it and saw the beer was all imported and the prices steep. It didn't make any sense to him to pay five dollars for any beer, no matter how far away the damned thing had been brewed. He turned a flap and saw a list of the specialty drinks. They offered every kind of cocktail you could imagine, including the house drink The Katrina. There was a picture of it and everything. Off to the side it sat, right next to the appetizers, tall and blue as any patch of water Billy had ever laid eyes on.

Underneath The Katrina was a sticker that looked like it'd just been pasted on. It was for a new drink called The Oil Spill. The description said it was a top-shelf Long Island Iced Tea with a little bit extra to get the bad taste out of your mouth. Billy looked up from the menu and saw The Oil Spill written all over the place in bright-colored chalk. It was there above the bar, over by the tables, in giant letters by the bathrooms.

While he was looking someone bumped into him and slipped up to the bar. He could see right away it was June. Her hair, done up so perfect, had fallen down from its bun and onto her shoulders. Sweat slicked her skin. She ordered a pair of cocktails, handed the bartender a bill, and slinked away.

Billy wanted to grab her right then. Spin her around and tell her the jig was up, that she needed to get home and get her shit and get to leaving, maybe even throw in his piece of mind for a minute or two, but he couldn't make himself do it and she walked right by him, close enough for him to smell the perfume he'd bought her for her last birthday. But he didn't lay a hand on her.

Instead, he watched her weave through the crowd and toward the outside patio. He watched her and followed. Past the men with expensive haircuts and women wearing gaudy jewelry. The tables of people laughing it up and kicking back their Katrinas and Oil Spills. He followed her to the patio where large fans whirred above everyone and sent the candle flames on the tables dancing.

They were toward the back, June and the businessman. She sat down next to him and settled into the crook of his beefy arm. He was older, late fifties maybe, and his hair was shock-white and combed back in a very proper fashion. He didn't look like much to Billy, not from what he could see, so Billy walked right up to the table.

June saw him first and sat right up and spilled her drink across the tablecloth. It leaked out all over their plates and silverware and pooled up around the base of the candle. The businessman didn't react as quickly. He wrapped his arm further around June and squeezed her with one of his big, spotted hands.

Billy wanted to say something, anything, but the words fumbled around in his mouth and got lost. He wanted to go on and on about lies and betrayal and the destruction of everything he loved. He wanted to tell her she'd gone and whored herself out for the last night. He wanted to tell her he'd never see her deceitful ass again. The look she gave him though was so small and pained he couldn't. It was the same one she'd given him out there on The Fly whenever they'd finished lovemaking and the weather turned cold. The same one she'd given him whenever she'd known she'd messed up. Back when she gave a goddamn.

It was enough for Billy to forgive her. He wanted to reach out and touch her hand, her small hand braced on the wet table. Then the businessman pulled her closer and laughed a little, showing that space between his teeth Billy had thought about so much. He reached with his other hand and grabbed a straw off the table and sunk it deep into his drink. He took a long draw and smiled.

Billy was on him then. Dove right over the table and sent the two of them rolling into the party just behind them. When he hit the ground Billy was aware right away that he'd banged his chest and knees pretty good going over and pain shot up to and through his arms. He didn't slow though, not even as each pound of his heart sent dull fire through him or as people scattered and yelled and screamed. Billy had the businessman down on the ground and he cinched up on his knees and got his arms pinned. That shit-eating grin was gone, and now Billy could see that gap as clear as day through the businessman's busted lips. He rained down on it, that gap, and drove and ground his fist into it until it broke away and he felt give.

The businessman tried to squirm his way free but Billy had too good of a hold. He got down low and elbowed him in the cheek and the side of his head. June stood off to the side, sobbing and screaming.

Billy, she yelled, but he continued sending blows like the ticking of a clock. Feeling give here and the crunch of bones there. He toured the businessman's face and felt his blood dripping off his own fists. He wiped them clean on the businessman's shirt and left dark red palm streaks up and down his chest.

Billy went on like that. His knuckles pounding, a few of them already shattered. The businessman went slack underneath, as loose as a puddle, but Billy couldn't stop. He checked out. Something inside him clicked and, somehow, in that gap of teeth, he could almost see those four men in shirts and ties from the TV standing in the dark. The hot breath of Louisiana beat down on their brows and begged sweat out of them. Like always they were shaking their heads and arguing where to point their fingers and who to blame. And Billy felt himself out there in the water, out in the Gulf, the Atlantic, out wherever, the waves lolling in and lifting him up and pushing him down, swarming around and drowning him as he beat his hands into the surf. By his feet were the boards of a wrecked ship, bobbing around like ice in a drink. Something was spreading out there, spreading like a pool, and it leaked up and blinded him and swelled in his chest while he beat at what lay before him. There was only black then, crude and bad intentions, the welling up of the bowels of the earth.

ALL THE
FAMILIAR PLACES

I only lived a couple of blocks away from the Prancing Pig, which was good because it was one of the few places in town a guy could go to lighten his head. It was a barbecue joint that doubled as a club and it had a long bar that ran from one end of the room to another with a whole wall of mirrors behind. Some nights, when the weather was nice and business had been good, they brought bands in to play and people came and danced and boozed 'til morning. I needed something like that, what with work and life being such motherfuckers, but I knew I wasn't going to be getting any relief that night. My friend Buster's wife had just left him and he needed someone to talk to. Buster was a big guy, probably six-five or so, built too, but he looked like a house that was just about ready to fall apart.

It's just about the most rotten deal you could imagine, he said, swirling his beer around in its mug. His eyes were shot to hell and every time he brought up his runaway wife his voice got this sad little hitch in it. I mean, goddamn, the guy's a manager out at the movie place. He sells popcorn. How could it get any worse?

I said I'd try not to think about it too much. At the time I was thirty and divorced, with a sweetheart I couldn't keep tabs on for anything. Every time I looked up she was out raising hell with some of the new pilots from the nearby Air Force base. I mean, I had my own problems to worry about.

Buster slammed his mug down on the bar and laughed. Last week she called just to tell me that she thought she'd confused her disgust of me for love, he said. That she doesn't know how she ever shared a bed with me in the first place. Ruthless stuff, you know? Saying things about my family and how terrible things were.

Christ, I said, half paying attention to him and half watching the drummer of the band that'd just finished up. He was lugging his equipment toward the door and the crowd of drunks was so bad he had to stop and wait for people to move out of his way. It wasn't anything I hadn't seen before, but it was better than talking about women and love.

Had my daughter on the phone yesterday, Buster said. Said she had some things to get off her chest. Like how she can see why her mom doesn't want anything to do with me and that I would be doing everyone a big favor if I just went and took a flying leap off the water tower. I swear, Shirley's got everyone believing her lies. Everyone.

The bartender brought over a couple more beers and set them down in front of us. Lord knows I needed one. Hearing Buster talk about his kid made me start thinking about my boy Aaron. He'd turned eight the week before and there'd been a party and everything, but I hadn't seen him in a year and a half and couldn't just drop in. Besides, the idea of sitting out back of my old house and watching my ex-wife kiss and hug my old buddy Stevie Johnson sounded like hell. It wasn't Aaron's fault though, and it was awful he had to suffer because of it.

But the worst part was having to think about Stevie, the same guy I'd been running around with for years, shacking up with my ex Cheryl. When it came down to it, I always had to look back on the times he'd been around her, those times we'd been out to eat, or watching a movie, and wonder if he was looking at her like that the whole time. Made me think about when we'd all come down to the Prancing Pig, especially near the end, when I'd spent the night dancing on the floor with Rebecca, my sweetheart, and the two of them had just sat in a booth talking. Trying to figure out if they were in love then or if it happened later got me real sick to my stomach.

I drained my beer in a couple of gulps and looked at Buster. He had his head down and his massive gut resting against the bar. Water was crawling down his cheeks.

You think kids hold grudges? I asked him. I mean, you think they'll look back when they're older and think their dads were just the worst sons of bitches they ever met?

Buster lifted his head and sucked up his tears. There ain't no way, he said. They get that old and they're gonna start understanding these things. He wiped his eyes with the back of his sleeve and then traced his finger across the rim of his mug. But I don't know, he said. I don't feel like I know one goddamn thing anymore.

We sat and stared at the crowd. The set was over, but that didn't mean the people were leaving. Every so often the door would open and a couple or two would stumble in, the boys holding up their ladies long enough to stuff them into an open table or booth. I was calling for another beer, but the bartender was at the other end of the bar talking to an old man in a red and black flannel. The old man was leaning across and it looked to me like he was jawing away. They were going at it for a while until the bartender came out from behind the bar and grabbed the old man by the arm and started pulling him toward the door. The old man fought, but he kept one of his arms carefully across his gut as if he were holding something there. Before too long the old man was outside and the bartender was back serving drinks.

When I asked him what happened he rolled his eyes and said, That guy's in here all the time selling shit and begging for free drinks. Last week he brought in a trash bag full of clothes and kept bugging everyone to buy some.

What'd he have tonight? I asked him.

Fucker brought a dog in here, the bartender said. You can't bring a fucking *dog* into a *bar*. Everybody knows that.

I asked him what kind of dog it was.

How would I know? he said.

Now, you have to know that sometimes I turn soft when I drink. Sure, most of the time I either get good and buzzed and head home, or I drink a few too many and look for somebody to thump, but sometimes I'll get to thinking about the past and the things I've lost and I'll start crying like a child. That night, hearing about the old man and his dog, I started thinking about a dog I'd had when I was a boy. I called him Jack and he was just about the best damn friend anyone ever had. Used to follow me all over town and slept at the foot of my bed every night. I got to thinking about how every boy should have a dog that good and true and how my boy, my one and only boy, didn't have any such dog and the thought hurt so bad I had to get a hold of myself before I started blubbering on like Buster.

After a while I couldn't stand it anymore and went looking for the old man. I figured he'd be long gone by the time I made it out the door, but he was sitting right there on a bench outside. He was smoking a cigarette and petting a bulge on his belly.

Heard you're looking to sell a dog, I said.

Did you? he said. You heard that?

How much? I said.

The old man leaned back against the building and exhaled long and slow. This here ain't nothin' but a pup, he said. Sweet lil' thing, too, and I ain't gonna sell him to someone who's gonna do him harm.

I took some bills out of my wallet and showed them to him. I don't wanna harm anything, I said. Just wanna take him back to my boy, that's all.

A couple of drunks came through the door and staggered down the sidewalk, dragging their feet the whole way, but when they were gone the old man looked to me and slowly unbuttoned his flannel. He ain't got no name, he said, but that don't mean he ain't worth a shit. Lots of things ain't got no name and they mean somethin', you know?

From inside the shirt came the dog's head. It was a blonde thing, a mutt no doubt, but I could tell by the way its little eyes kept darting around it was going to be a hell of a dog.

He's a good lookin' boy, ain't he?

Yeah, I said. Damned right he is.

The old man stood up and took my money. Now, he said, I want your word you're gonna take care of this here puppy, all right?

You got my word, I said. I'm gonna take care of this dog like he was family.

He cradled the dog to his chest and stroked it. Right then that dog seemed to be the most important thing in his life and, for a moment, I didn't know if he was going to hand it over to me or not. All right, he said, pushing it toward me. You take care now, all right, you take care and be good.

It was around three in the morning and I knew it would be better if I just took him home and waited to give him to Aaron, but I was so excited that I knew I wasn't gonna be able to sleep. I figured it wouldn't be so bad if I walked over there right then and introduced my boy to his new best friend. What was the harm in it, really? I was in the tank already and the idea sounded like a real winner.

So that dog and me went for a walk. We started off down the street and toward my old house. The sky was just pitch black and there wasn't a person to be found anywhere. All the lights to all the houses were off and all the cars were parked along the curbs. There was hardly a sound, save for the crickets and the occasional train passing through. It was just me and the *tick-tick-tick-tick* of the dog's nails on the blacktop. Maybe it was just me, but he seemed more than happy to be walking around. He kept trotting down the street, farther and farther, until I could barely see him at all and had to get after him. But like the good dog he was, he'd come right back and walk alongside me.

A mile or so and we were there. The place was a neat little brick house with green shutters. On the porch was a swing I'd put up a few years before. The only things different from when I'd left was a flag that'd been hung and a bike lying out in the wet grass. It felt like it used to whenever I'd come home from the bars, only I knew it wasn't my house or life anymore.

I picked the dog up from the sidewalk and carried him to the door. I knocked and for a while there wasn't an answer, but after a minute or two the lights turned on and I could hear someone working the chain lock. Then, standing there in the doorway with nothing but his skivvies on, was my old buddy Johnson. In his hand was the same ball bat I'd always kept under the bed, just in case.

What in the hell? he said, rubbing the sleep out of his eyes. Jim, just what in the hell are you doing here?

I nodded at the dog in my arms and smiled. Figured the boy could use a dog, I said.

Cheryl came up behind him, clutching her housecoat closed. She looked confused. Steve, she said. Who is it? What's the matter?

It's Jim, he said. He turned to her and dropped the ball bat. Something about a dog.

Jim? she said. Is everything all right? Are you drunk?

I was gonna say no, but I figured after eight years of marriage it wasn't going to be that easy to lie, so I shrugged and lifted the dog up for her to see. I said, He doesn't have a name, but I think he's great anyway. Besides, Aaron can think of a real good name for him.

Jim, she said. It's almost four in the morning. You can't just come over like this and bring a dog with you.

We stood there for a few seconds without saying anything. Just me with the dog and them standing in the doorway trying to wake up. I almost left before Cheryl cleared her throat.

You want to come in for some coffee? she said. Sit down and sober up a bit?

I followed Stevie into the kitchen while Cheryl went to get dressed. The layout hadn't changed a bit, not in the slightest. There was my old living room with the same leather couch and chair my ma and dad had bought us for our first Christmas, the dining room table we used to eat at every Sunday evening, and even the movie cabinet I'd made with my own two hands was where I'd left it.

Stevie and me took a seat at the kitchen table and had nothing better to do than sit there and look at each other while the puppy ran around. My old buddy was starting to look heavy. His cheeks were rounder and his stomach hung over the waist of his pajamas. It was strange because, for as long as I could remember, Stevie had always been as lean and mean as a stick.

Say, I said, trying to break the ice. How about I go and wake Aaron up, huh? It'd be a big surprise. Happy birthday, and all that.

Stevie got up to put a pot of coffee on. He's not here, he said, pushing the buttons on the machine. He's staying the night over at his grandma's.

It made sense, what he was saying, but I was having a hell of a time wrapping my drunk head around the words. Wait, you mean he's not here? I said.

He sat back down and sighed. That's what I mean, he said.

Cheryl came in wearing an undershirt and joined us. It seemed so familiar, us sitting at the table together and her in one of those shirts. Used to be she always wore mine and I'd get pissed whenever I opened my dresser and found they were all gone. I'd say something like, Save me one, why don't you? Seeing her, though, in a big shirt that was obviously Stevie's was real sad. Its neck was all stretched out and it hung from her like a dress.

We sat there watching the dog walk around and sniff everything. When the coffee finished Cheryl poured out three cups and put some sugar and milk on the table.

You got any food for him? I said, pointing to the dog. You could see his ribs poking out and he looked like he was about ready to starve to death. I doubt he's had a lick to eat in a while, I said.

Sorry, Stevie said. We didn't expect anybody to bring a dog by at three in the morning.

I looked at him, my old buddy from way back. For the longest time I couldn't believe he'd taken up with my girl and moved into my house. Sitting there, stirring some milk into my coffee, I could hardly recognize him at all.

Cheryl got up and went to the refrigerator. Hold on, she said. I think we've got some cold cuts. She pulled out a plastic sack and tore up some meat into little pieces and laid it in front of the dog. It gave the meat a sniff and gobbled it up, his tail wagging like mad the whole time.

When she sat back down, Cheryl seemed happy the dog was eating. A smile spread across her face and right then she looked as beautiful as I'd ever seen her. Sure, she'd always been a pretty girl, but late in our lives together she'd given up and stopped caring. For days on end she wouldn't wash her hair or put on a lick of makeup. She was the kind of girl who could get away with it, but the lack of upkeep coupled with the great sadness she carried around was too much. The night we'd agreed to a separation she'd looked as old as a grandmother. Now she had the life back in her.

How're things? she said to me.

Nothin' to complain about, I said.

Still running round with Rebecca?

Honestly, I said, I don't know if I could tell you. Sometimes it seems like we're together and ready to settle down, but then she just up and disappears. Goes missing for a couple of days.

That's too bad, Cheryl said. She leaned back in her chair and took a long, satisfied drink of her coffee. Maybe when she grows up a little she'll be ready to settle, she said.

There was nothing more for me to say, so I just nodded. I looked up and Stevie was nursing his drink and shooting me daggers. The only time he ever looked away was to check the time on the clock above the sink. He didn't want me there, and I couldn't blame him.

What's this about Aaron being over at your mom's? I said.

Hell, she said, he's over there more than he's not anymore. You know Mom and Dad. They just spoil him and let him get away with everything. For his birthday they brought over a carful of presents. Stacked up they were taller than him.

I meant to make it over here for that one, I lied.

I know it's hard, she said. But, Jim, he's the only boy you got.

Stevie laughed. C'mon, he said. Did you forget who you're talking to? Hell, we've got the Father of the Year sittin' here. He doesn't need any advice on raising a kid.

That's enough, Cheryl said.

I looked down at the puppy again. He was smelling my shoes and his tail was just a going. He looked up at me with those big, black eyes of his and I could tell he was going to be the best dog my boy would ever have. Listen, I said. I had a dog when I was a kid. Damn good dog, too.

His name was Jack, Cheryl said. Right?

That's the one, I said. And I think you could do a whole lot worse than to name this here little one after him.

Aaron can name his own damn dog, Steve said. He's plenty capable.

Cheryl nodded and reached her arm around the shoulders of her new husband. I like it, she said. It sounds about right.

I knew I'd outstayed my welcome so I leaned down and patted the dog one last pat on the head. It wagged its tail a little more and then went bounding into the other room. As I was walking to the door Cheryl made me promise I'd come and see Aaron before too long, and I said I would, not knowing if I was telling the truth or not. When the time came I went ahead and shook Steve's hand, but neither one of us put much into it. Some things just go away, I guess.

I got outside and saw morning was coming on. Some birds were singing in the trees. The lights went out in the house behind me and I was left alone on the porch. Beer was still thudding around in my head so I took a seat on the swing and looked out at the street. Some of the cars were still the same and the neighbors had their trash cans out in all the spots they'd had them years before. The whole damned place looked exactly how I left it.

So I sat there, looking at all those cars from my past and getting my head about me, watching the day roll in and wash the black out with its sad shade of blue. In a couple of hours the paperboy rode through on his bike and his hat tried to fly right off his head. A city truck was behind him. It stopped in the street in front of me and a couple of city men jumped down and emptied the cans into their truck. When they were done they tossed them back onto the sidewalk. Before they took off I felt like running up and grabbing one of those handles on the side and riding that truck wherever, across town, the state, maybe even all the way out to California, moving from morning back to the night, and letting go whenever I was good and ready. I thought about going somewhere, anywhere but there, and starting up something, something real and true. I thought about it, good and long, but, by the time I talked my legs into it that truck was hulking down the line to the next block, leaving only smoke behind.

NOW I AM BECOME DEATH, DESTROYER OF WORLDS

I used to beg my daddy to take me along when he went fishing. Every time he loaded up the car and left his rods by the door for the night I'd get on my knees and cry myself hoarse. That went on for years until one day, God knows why, he said okay.

Morning of he got me out of bed around four to get ready. When I got to the kitchen there were some pancakes on the table and Daddy was loading up one of his toolboxes with beers from the fridge. When we finished up we got in the truck and headed for the lake. Daddy was a patrol man for the city and he liked listening to detective dramas on the radio. Wherever we went we'd listen to one. We always caught them in the middle and didn't ever really know what was going on or what the story was.

That day we heard a good part of one. The drive to the lake took a half hour or so and we listened the whole way. The story went something like this: a woman had married a man she hardly knew and, a year into the thing, he disappeared with all her money and valuables. The detective found the guy, but he got away after a long chase through a meatpacking plant. Here's the thing though—he didn't just escape and stay gone. No. He went back and beat that woman to death with a hammer. Beat her until she wasn't even recognizable.

Now, that just drove me crazy. I couldn't figure out at the time why somebody would kill someone else. The whole thing seemed cruel and awful. So I asked my daddy about it. I asked how things like that could happen. Daddy turned down the radio and got himself a cigarette out of his pack.

I don't know what to tell you, he said. He took a puff and turned the volume back up.

We got to the boat ramp and got in line behind a couple of guys in matching vests. The lake was famous for its trout and there wasn't a summer day it wasn't crowded. It was worth it though. Those fish were big and heavy and they snapped at anything you put in the water. Daddy cussed up a storm and blamed tourism and the rich folks who came down from the city, but we waited our turn just the same.

By the time we got in the water the sun was out in full and the heat was terrible. Soon as we got good and going Daddy pulled out some beers and slurped them down. Half the time he was more concerned with drinking than his line. But he put his beer down the second I got a bite. It fought and made a run or two, but once he got his hands on that rod Daddy reeled it in quick as shit. He pulled it out of the water and held it up like it was some kind of trophy or something. It was a two-foot skinny thing with a torn fin and dead eyes.

Goddamn it, Daddy said. Ain't worth eating and it ain't worth saving.

Daddy grabbed it under the head and slammed it against one of the boat seats. He got a knife out of his tackle box and jammed it so far in the trout's head it hit the aluminum. When it was over he tossed the trout back in the water and cleaned the knife off on his jeans. The blood and brains were like black snot.

The day moved on and between the two of us we'd hauled in a pretty respectable cash. Our cooler was full and couldn't even hold one more, but we stayed out there and drifted awhile. Daddy still had a couple of beers left and the temperature had dropped a bit. There wasn't much said. Daddy never said much anyway. But at one point, when we'd reeled in our lines and were putting new bait on our hooks, he turned and spit over the side.

You asked about killin', he said. And I'll tell you somethin' about it if you even wanna know. I said I did and waited while he dug into a cup of dirt for a worm. The one he pulled out was fat and pink. The shit that goes on, he said, it's enough to make a guy sick. He tore the worm in half and dropped part of it back in the dirt. I've had these problems with my stomach, he said. Got a hole in there that bleeds and they say it's from worry and fear.

I threaded my worm onto my line and casted as fast as I could. I didn't have the heart to see them squirm.

Last week we got a call, he said. He got his bait ready like it was nothing. His hands squeezed that worm onto the barb and twisted the next link on too. Then the next and the next, juices running over the pads of his fingers. Domestic, he said. Guy was all hopped up on something and causing a fuss.

Daddy took a drink and wiped his mouth with the back of his hand. He was looking at his hook and his worm. He said,

We get there and he's talkin' crazyshit. Saying he was the truth and the way. That he had broke through and seen the face of God. And his wife is on the floor crying and throwin' up. Going on and on about the kitchen. About her little boy. Well, we went in there and there's this boy in there. Four years old. Looked just like you when you were that age. Blonde hair, like yours before it changed, and wearing this basketball shirt and shorts.

Daddy got out another beer and drained the last drop out of the can he was drinking. He cast his line and it looped, way up high and into the air, a perfect arc, and landed with a plop out in the middle of the water.

I couldn't get over it, he said. Just how much he looked like you. It was hard to be in there. I wanted to pick him up and take him home he looked the part so much. But it wasn't right. Something wasn't right. He was walking around in circles all drunk-like. Stumbling and talking nonsense.

A second passed and Daddy cranked his reel and pulled in his line.

His daddy was all hopped up and tossed him at the cabinet, he said. When Daddy got the line in the worm was already gone. He laughed and took his pole apart. I don't know, he said. When you get down to it, maybe some sons of bitches deserve to die.

We got home just as it turned dark. Inside Mom was fixing canned spaghetti on the stove and making some instant lemonade. Daddy and me had a glass and went outside to clean our fish. I did as my daddy said and put a couple of trout on his work bench. They were still alive and kicking. It took all I had to keep them from wiggling off. Daddy came and drove a nail through each of their heads. That didn't kill them either. They kept going.

You ever skin one? he said. The trick is to get a good grip.

He got a pair of pliers from another toolbox and clamped down its teeth. Then you peel it, he said and yanked a paper-like layer off the fish. I could see its flesh and it was white.

Get a seam, he said, pressing a knife into the meat. Pare away as much as you can, carve out the organs, and cut at an angle. The knife drove into the fish's head and clipped it off. Here, he said, handing me the pliers. Get you one.

I took them but felt bad. The fish still in the toolbox were jumping around and gulping for air. I thought the one on the board was hissing at me.

There a problem? Daddy said after I took too long in start-ing.

I wanted to say no, no problem at all, and tear into it. I wanted to yank and cut and be done with it. But I couldn't make myself.

In a little while Daddy got tired and pointed to the fish. Tell you what, he said. You're not comin' in 'til you clean. This is my house and I'll be fucked if I let a pussy sleep here. He wiped his hands on his pants and went inside. When the door closed I heard the lock click shut. After a few hours I knew he wasn't going to let it drop.

The first cut I said sorry the whole way. Sorry fish, I said. But all it did was open its mouth and try and breathe. I walked away. I thought maybe the thing would just snuff out on its own. Just stop. But it didn't. It kept trying to breathe and I couldn't wait no more.

Mom was still stirring in the kitchen. She had the radio on like usual and was listening to one of those old choirs. They were singing about providence, saying things like just wait, that son of God's gonna come and make all the wrongs right. She was singing and looked out at me and we caught eyes. She looked away.

I traced the knife to the lines on the trout. Throat to stomach and so on. I lifted them out like string and tossed them on the floor. I cut until there wasn't nothing to cut. I touched the walls and felt the give, I fingered until there was nothing but scales.

By the third or fourth it was nothing. I lifted out the guts and squished them like jelly. I flipped them at the walls and watched them slide down.

Real.

Slow.

Like.

Supper was ready when I went in and Mom had our TV trays set up around the living room. Daddy had on a show about the coming reckoning, our Lord in Savior Jesus Goddamn Christ, he said, ready to come back and whip some ass.

Wash your hands, Mom said.

I went in the bathroom to do just that, but after I turned on the water and got the soap out of the closet I stopped and took a big smell. All my fingers smelled like fish and blood and I'll be damned if it didn't smell just like life and summer and I ran the water and didn't even bother putting them under.

We sat around and watched that TV. The preacher said there were signs wherever you looked. Volcanoes, sickness, a star or two streaking across the black night. God, in all his glorious anger, is angry and ready to balance the scales. My daddy nodded and ate big forkfuls of Mom's spaghetti and washed it down with what was left of his beer. Hallelujah, he said. Reckoning, he said. And I sat twiddling my fork with one hand and brushing the other past my nose. Somewhere, deep back there, I was like those fish, swimming past the breakers, shimmering down the channels and dams, moving just as fast as the light hitting the surface. I was punching my way through, making my way out to the coast and breaking into that waterway, seeing the sun and the loving eyes of my creator. And I didn't have a doubt right then. I knew it well as I knew myself. There was nothing gonna ever stand in my way again.

NIGHT OF THE REVOLUTION

The night of the revolution I pulled my baby out of bed and told her to stay low to the floor. I could hear gunfire in the distance so I grabbed my rifle from the closet and threw on some clothes and shoes and went out to get a better handle on things.

Down the street marched a bunch of neighbors armed with whatever'd been handy. Some were carrying pieces of wood and extension cords. I could tell by the way their faces looked in the orange glow of the street lights that they meant business. They were yelling and carrying on, talking about justice and comeuppance.

My neighbor Freddy had a pistol in one hand and an axe handle in the other. Hey Freddy, I said. What the hell we got here?

Freddy uncocked his pistol and walked the couple of feet from his lawn to mine. Fuck if I know, he said.

The two of us merged into the foot traffic and followed it downtown. There were patrol cars parked at every intersection but no one behind the wheels. The lights they left on were flashing against the buildings and the people and they made everything look purple.

Around Roosevelt I heard the group up ahead start into a cheer. They kept saying fuck the greed and other things of that nature. Then it turned to find the pigs and all the faces around me started turning ugly and mean. A few broke from the march and ran into the Meadow Springs gated community. They had bicycle chains and crowbars and ball bats and they sprinted past the lighted guard booth and disappeared around the block.

A helicopter flew overhead and for a minute its big hot searchlight washed over us. There were some voices up there coming through a speaker system. The voices said go home, go home, but some of us started tossing chunks of sidewalk up toward the light. After while the chopper peeled out and curled around a line of buildings.

People were singing songs I hadn't heard since I was a kid. Songs on stations my mom used to listen to while she cooked breakfast. Songs about charity and the chance to do something worthwhile. Songs about unions and jobs suited for tough sons of bitches. So I slung my rifle over my shoulder and sang along like I was Dusty Springfield or something. Head back and shoulders straight.

We saw the bodies when we got near the business district. First one was hanging from a tree in front of a manicured yard. Then every couple of blocks you'd see a few more swinging from a street light or a lamp post. They swung back and forth and the ones that hung low enough we reached up and slapped their expensive loafers. Most had pieces of paper taped to them that said things like Traitor or Pig or Greed.

Stepping into Jewelry Row we bashed windows and trampled the broken glass under our feet. A couple of us went after the banks and ATMs. We got big handfuls of twenties and tossed them into the air. The paper mixed with the smoke rolling in from elsewhere and it was like snow as we moved forward.

By four we had City Hall and county lockup surrounded. We took turns throwing bricks at the doors and windows. Like children we paraded around the building and yelled for whoever was inside to get it over with and come on out. Some dropped their jeans and masturbated furiously. They howled and cried and whooped and hollered. Time dragged on and we got the sense We were winning and They were losing.

I thought about my dad then. I thought of when he used to get home from the chair plant and look out the window to our backyard. Used to sit there for an hour or so and work the kinks out of his arthritic hands. He'd shake his head and tell me how everything crooked in this world rose to the top and stayed there. That someday there was gonna be one helluva reckoning.

The whole thing got me choked up to no end. I grabbed Freddy and the guy next to me by the arm and got to dancing. My feet were moving and I could feel my face hot like a flame. Damn the bastards, I said. Damn them all to hell.

We all got going, every last one of us. The machinists and farmers and waitresses and factory help, the whole goddamn bunch of us danced and yelped and acted the fool. The boys in lockdown squeezed their heads through the bars in the windows and joined right in. They said get at it, burn this motherfucker right down to the ground.

I was really feeling it then, my feet kicking and voice singing up to those boys in the cells. I turned to Freddy and said how about it, huh? And Freddy said hell yes, his eyes big and his smile bright. I thought he was so beautiful, and the next second his head rocked back and a cloud of pink shot from his brow. His body fell backward and damn near dragged me down with it. A few others got hit too and pretty soon everyone was crying and running behind cars and mailboxes for cover.

Goddamn sniper, someone yelled.

Fella's up on top of the Wabash Building, said another.

Shots were raining down and hitting every which way. I got on the ground and crawled over to a corner where a bunch of people were hiding.

Sonuvabitch, a man nearby said. Gonna kill every last one of us.

I listened to the bullets wheeling by and got something of a bead on the shooter. He was between the fourth and eighth floors, and I could see, just barely, the open window he was aiming out of. Every so often I saw a flash come from there.

Now, I'm no hero, never been accused, but something came over me and I made a line past the boxes and cars and into the lobby of the Wabash. Things were a mess inside. Seeing as it served as a hub for every fat cat and lawyer in town, it wasn't a surprise. There were bodies piled on the floor and puddles of blood pooling in the center. I saw a man with a caved-in head slumped behind the receptionist's desk. Next to him was some bald bastard in a pinstriped suit. His throat had been plum torn out.

Something drove me on. I ran up the first four flights and checked there. Nothing, so I kept going. At the next landing I found a good-looking woman in a sweater and slacks. She was soaked through with sweat. Her makeup was streaked.

Please, she said, grabbing at my leg. Please get me out of here. I'm *innocent*.

Innocent? I said.

Sure, she said. I pay my taxes. I sit in the First Church of Christ every Sunday and pray for forgiveness. I clip coupons from the Sunday paper. My mother lives in the hungry part of town and worked every day of her life to give me everything she didn't have.

There wasn't anything I could do. I nodded, but didn't offer a hand. People gotta lie in the bed they made. My daddy taught me that much.

Up by the seventh floor I heard the punch of rifle fire. I pushed open the door and crawled into the hallway. The alarms were going off and the lights were flashing. Up and down the hall there were people lying everywhere, their eyes still open.

I followed the sound over to Room 728. The door was cracked and I could see the shooter squatting next to the window, his weapon on his shoulder.

Somehow I managed to kick open the door and rush in. He was so taken he was slow to turn and I tackled him. Both of our rifles fell and skittered over to the wall. The office was filled with paper and files and spent shells. I socked him in the mouth and he sent one right back. He gave me a good knee in the balls before I got a hold of his wrists and cinched up his legs with mine. I butted my head into his nose and right away his eyes started watering and blood ran down his mouth and over his chin. He was an ugly one with eyebrows that ran together and a mug that looked like it'd been through a windshield a time or two. There was a tag on his shirt that said his name was Billy.

I lowered my face down to his and smelled the whiskey on his lips. Something kicked around inside me and I started crying something awful. Big drops of water rolling down my face, falling onto his.

Goddamn it, I said. Goddamn it.

He tried to turn, but I kept him in place. The blood was running from his nose and over his big fat neck.

I've lost everyone and everything that ever meant fuckall to me, he said. My wife is loose and my work is gone. There isn't a thing in this God-forsaken world left for me.

I slapped him and felt his blood over the back of my hand. He sniveled and cried and I kissed him full on the lips. I wiped the sweat from his brow. I got close. Our wet faces touched.

You dumb sonuvabitch, I said. We gotta find some truth. Don't you know we gotta find some goddamn truth?

AN END
TO ALL THINGS

The signs showed up overnight. One day they weren't there and the next they were everywhere, these big black billboards with a date and the words An End to All Things. Everyone talked about them at work. Some people thought maybe it was a book or a movie. Others said it was just a stunt of some kind. It wasn't until my wife Jess called that afternoon that we found out what the deal was.

It's a cult, she said. I could already hear her getting excited. They're talking about it on the news right now, she said.

A cult, I said, I didn't know anything about a cult.

They're called the Brotherhood of the Last Revelation, Jess said. They've set up shop over at the old Quick Lube building. Their leader's this guy named Brother James and he's talking like God put them up to it.

It wasn't a surprise that Jess had gotten down to the bottom of the situation. She had strange interests, strange hobbies. For a while there it was telling fortunes and she'd make me sit down so she could practice on me. After that it was World War II. Or, more particular, the Nazis and the occult and concentration camps. I never got it, never understood for a second, but I kept my mouth shut and let her do her thing. She must've watched every show on the subject and read every book. She jumped headfirst into things like that. So it didn't shock me at all that she had the scoop on those billboards.

What about the date? I said. That when all hell breaks loose?

You got it, she said. And it's not too far off either. So I suggest picking up some canned goods on your way home.

When I got there she was camped out on the couch with a bowl of cherries in her lap. She still had on the scrubs she always wore to work. Look at this, she said and pointed to the TV. They're running specials about the end of the world. This one's about this tribe in the 1st century that said we're living in the end times.

Onscreen was this fella in a big feather headdress. His chest was covered with white, painted symbols. Under him was a guy tied to a rock. He was trying to get free. The fella with the headdress, the witch doctor, was chanting and waving around this dagger. Then, out of nowhere, he stabbed the other guy in the stomach and started dipping his hands in the blood.

They said the world was gonna be swallowed by fire, Jess said, popping a cherry into her mouth. She chewed and spit its pit back into the bowl. They said every now and then a big change comes along, she said.

Jesus, I said.

She said, Crazy right? and resituated on the couch. Funny thing is, she said, there's this other guy that saw into the future—

Nostradamus? I said.

No, she said, getting annoyed. I know who Nostradamus is. Why wouldn't I know who Nostradamus is?

I backed off at that point because I knew that's the way fights with us always started. She'd misunderstand something I'd said and get going like there was no tomorrow. It'd go on and on until she was a tear-soaked mess and we'd forgotten just what we'd been fighting about in the first place. Happened every time, but I'd learned my lesson. I figured out it was in my best interest just to stop. Just to say whatever it was I thought she wanted to hear and avoid the whole damn mess altogether.

Tell me about this guy, I said.

It doesn't matter, she said, looking back at the TV. I guess it doesn't matter when you really get down to it.

She stopped then and I didn't push. I figured if she wanted to talk she would. And she did after the show moved on to people who'd been so sure the end was coming that they'd killed themselves off. That's when she started back up.

This guy, she said, would hypnotize himself—

How'd he manage that? I said. I was half-paying attention to the show and this cult that'd killed themselves. They were lying in a field, dead, lying in circles and holding hands. How do you hypnotize yourself? I said

What does it matter? Jess said. She put her bowl down on the coffee table with a bang. I mean, really. What does it matter how he hypnotized himself? He hypnotized himself.

Okay, I said. Okay.

Anyway, she said. He hypnotized himself all the time and he'd have these dreams about wars and diseases and all those things. She paused and leaned forward to pick out a cherry. There was another cult on the show, this one with all its people dead and lying in bunk beds. Jess said, I mean this guy predicted us going to the moon and the internet. And he said the end was going to come in our lifetime. He didn't have a doubt in his mind.

How about that, I said and got up to go to the kitchen. I'd had enough dead people and sacrifices. It'd been a long day and I'd put up with enough that I didn't want to come home and put up with that apocalypse shit. All I wanted was some food. I got up and went into the kitchen to get a leftover steak out of the fridge, but a calendar stuck on the door caught my eye. Jess had circled the date from the billboards and written An End to All Things under it in big red letters.

I heated up that steak and popped a squat on the couch next to Jess. While I was eating she watched something about these foreign children, orphans, who'd been visited by the ghost of the Virgin Mary. Seems like ol' Mary told them a lot about what was going to happen in the future and how it was all gonna go down. Didn't sound like too good a news from the way they were talking about it.

Hey, I said to Jess. Any chance we can give this a rest for awhile? Maybe turn on the news for a minute or two? At least until I'm done eating?

She didn't like it, but she did it all the same. And, sure enough, the first story was about those goddamn signs. Jess turned to me and smiled in a way that about drove me up the wall. They were interviewing people on the news and asking what they thought and everyone pretty much agreed that it was a crock and a waste of time, but there were some who said that maybe it was the real deal.

You never know, said a woman out front of the Shop N Save. She had a cartful of groceries and two lost-looking kids trailing behind. One of these days it's all going to end, she said. Why not now?

Listen to her, Jess said with a laugh. Can you believe it?

I was about to tell her just how much I couldn't believe it, but she shushed me. She did it because there, on camera, was Brother James, the leader of the Brotherhood of the Last Revelation. He was an old, thin guy with a wooly beard that didn't cross above his lips and he was wearing a cheap tan suit and a badly tied blue tie. He had missing teeth and an accent so thick you could barely understand him. We did it 'cause we had to, he said. Lord tol' us to git e'ryone ready. He tol' us to git e'ryone ready and that's what we inten' to do.

He tol' 'em, Jess squealed. She slapped my leg. God done and tol' 'em, she said.

The report went on, but neither of us listened much. I was bored and Jess grabbed her computer off the floor and got to work looking up Brother James. When enough time passed that I knew we weren't gonna talk anymore, I flipped through the channels and settled on a game. My Pacers were playing Milwaukee and losing bad. I watched a bit and let Jess do her thing, but I got even more bored and just turned it off. I put the remote down and told her I was heading to bed.

Okay, she said, the glow off her computer on her face. Be there in a few.

When I got upstairs I undressed and pulled the covers over me. I looked at the bright numbers on the alarm clock and tried to sleep. All I could think about though was that witch doctor stabbing that fella on the rock. I thought about how much that would hurt, getting cut like that, and I rolled around a bit. It got so bad I almost called for Jess, but it wouldn't have mattered.

She'd turned the TV back on at that point and was watching another one of those shows. I didn't think she would've heard me for all the screams and explosions.

———

Back then Jess worked at this doctor's office on the outside of town. She answered calls and checked people in. She was also in charge of the nurses and assistants. A day didn't go by that she didn't talk shit about one, or all, of those girls. One gave her grief over everything. Another nurse never talked. The rest pissed her off about this or that. But there was one assistant named Michelle that really got to her.

She's a piece of work, Jess told me once. She walks around like she's every man's dream. And she always wants an audience. Doesn't matter what she's doing.

That was a regular thing, her bitching about Michelle and the rest of the girls at the office. So I didn't get it when she wanted to go to a party with the lot of them a couple of weeks later.

I thought you hated them, I said, not wanting to go. There was a big game on, not to mention it was the night before the day the world was supposed to end and I was sick to death of hearing about it. Why would you wanna spend a second more with these people than you have to? I said.

Because I always say no, she said, almost in tears. And if I keep saying no they're gonna stop asking.

That made sense. Jess and me had stopped going out for the most part. Couldn't afford it. In the past we'd had a whole group we'd gone out with for drinks and dinners, but somehow that'd dried up. We couldn't quite put our fingers on it, but we figured it might've been because we'd said no one too many times.

But why tonight? I said. There's a game on. Why's it gotta be tonight?

There's always a game on, she said.

Games are only on Tuesdays and Wednesdays and Fridays, I said.

There's a game on almost every night, she said and went into the kitchen. When she came back she had that calendar and was pointing at the date and the big red letters she'd written. There's a game on most every night, she said with a smile, but there's only one night before the planet blows up.

I groaned and that just got her started on how we never went anywhere or did anything. And I said okay, that's true, and the next thing I knew I was being pushed upstairs and into the shower. Jess stood in the bathroom, at the mirror, and got to work putting on her makeup. I could tell she was happy and that made the whole thing feel a little better. It'd been a long damn time since she'd seemed that happy about anything.

Seemed like once upon a time the two of us couldn't have been anymore pleased than we were, just being together and shooting the shit. And making love. By that night, the night of the party, we hadn't done that in so long I couldn't remember the last time. It wasn't like we'd made a decision to stop or talked it over or anything. It just stopped one day.

Hey, I said to her. You wanna jump in the shower maybe? Could be like old times.

In there? she said and laughed. Honey, I've got make-up on and my hair's already done. Maybe another time? she said.

Sure, I said. I wasn't that disappointed I guess. There was always a reason not to fool around then. Always something a little more pressing.

When I got out she'd laid one of my suits across the bed and a pair of wingtip shoes I never wore. They hurt my feet something awful.

The wingtips? I called to her. She was still in the bathroom.

They look good on you, she said, peeking around the corner. She was more done up than I'd seen her in a long while.

Within the hour we were in the car and headed to the party. It was raining hard and water flooded the street. That didn't stop the freaks from coming out though. They were all over the place, on the corners and at the lights, dressed in robes and holding signs that said things like The End is Near, Be Prepared and SEEK FORGIVENESS NOW. Jess ate all that up and laughed every time she saw a new one.

Isn't this just the greatest? she said.

Just the greatest, I said.

Everywhere I'd been I'd heard about those billboards and the crazies surrounding them. Work. The store. The bar. I couldn't get away. I didn't want to talk about it. I turned on the radio and went through the channels and it seemed like all the stations had the same idea and were playing songs about doomsday or how it was the end of the world and someone felt fine.

Goddamn, I said aloud.

Relax, Jess said, still searching the streets for more signs and more people. Hey, she said, pointing at a liquor store. We've gotta pick up some booze.

I pulled the car into the parking lot and Jess and me ran through the rain and to the door. There was even a sign on the window advertising some sale called the Beer-pocalypse.

Where's this party, anyway? I said, following Jess through the aisles. What kind of party are you dragging me to?

You're not going to like it, she said. She was choosing between vodkas. What kind of booze, she said, says I'm ready to go out with a bang?

I said, What'd you mean I'm not going to like it?

You're not going to like it, she said and decided on a bottle. What it is. Where it is. You're just not going to be happy about any of it.

I watched Jess go up to the register and pay. I knew right then where we were going.

It's at Doc's house, I said.

Doc, she said and handed me the six-pack I'd picked out. Why do you have to call him that?

What about it? I said.

You don't like him, Jess said as we walked out of the store and back into the rain. She waited until we got on the road to finish. You never liked Dr. Stevenson, she said.

She was right. I'd never liked Doc. Something always rubbed me wrong about the guy. It was something about the way he carried himself, or how he looked at Jess and all the other girls. Or how he had his house set up, full from top to bottom with every overpriced gadget and item he could stuff in there. Like he was trying to impress somebody.

Ever since that cookout, Jess said, you've had it out for him. Ever since he beat you at swimming and wouldn't give you a rematch.

In a way she was dead-on and in another she couldn't have been more off. I'd disliked him since she got hired on at the office and I saw him wheeling out in his brand new, cherry red Corvette. But he hadn't outraced me in the pool. I'd challenged him to the end and back after he spent the whole day prancing around and talking up the girls. I challenged him and I'd swear on my life I got him by a hair, but I'd kicked up such a wake in my stroke that everybody watching, Jess included, thought he got the best of me. The whole thing about killed me, watching him climb out and strut around like he was hot shit.

I'm just saying, I said to Jess, if he beat me then he wouldn't of minded another go.

Whatever, Jess said. There's just no reason to hate him like you do.

I don't hate him, I said, lying. I just don't love him like you do.

I don't love him, Jess said.

We got to Doc's house not long after. It was in a subdivision called Easy Acres, where the town's rich folks lived. All the houses were huge and made out of brick and they had columns and circular driveways out front.

You ready to go in? Jess said, grabbing her bottle.

I reckon, I said.

Please, she said. All I'm asking is that you don't cause some kind of scene.

No scene, I said.

As we walked up the door opened for us and Doc was standing there in a full tuxedo. He had his hair parted in this real dramatic way and a pipe clenched between his teeth. You could tell he was already three sheets to the wind.

What kind of party is this? I said to Jess.

You'll see, she said.

Welcome, welcome, Doc said. He reached out and shook my free hand. Then he turned to Jess. Lady Jessica, he said, kissing her cheek. Come in, make yourself at home. We only have a few hours to live, after all.

The house was filled with people standing around, talking and drinking. I recognized the girls Jess worked with and I watched her go to each of them and say hello. Doc took my coat and led me over to a corner where he had a book and a poster set up. The poster, tacked up next to a fireplace, was a picture of a mushroom cloud reaching toward the sky. Above the cloud were black letters that said An End to All Things. Nearby was a camera on a tripod, ready to take pictures.

The book, Doc said, pointing to a guest book on the mantle, is so there'll be something left behind for whatever future society digs us out of the ashes. He laughed and handed me a pen. So, you know, make sure it's good, he said.

Then he left me alone and went to put our things away. I flipped through the book and saw where people had written things like Brother James Wuz Here. Someone else had put down Dear Future, Do you have flying cars yet? When I looked up, Jess was standing in front of the poster, in front of the mushroom cloud. She was pretending to be terrified while Doc manned the camera.

Looks like you spared no expense, I said to him as he pressed a button.

No doubt about it, he said, showing Jess the camera and the picture. I mean, tomorrow's the big day. Best not leave anything on the table.

Jess and him laughed like that was just about the funniest thing ever. I laughed too and tried to play nice. I even joined in when they started talking about some kind of super volcano that could wipe out life.

That'd just about do it, Jess said. One of those goes off and you can forget about it.

No doubt, Doc said. Watched a show the other day that said there's one under Yellowstone. If that thing acts up you'd better say goodbye.

And it's overdue, Jess said, sipping a drink. We're on borrowed time as it is.

No doubt, I said, trying to make conversation. Her and Doc looked at me like I was interrupting, like I wasn't welcome. So I excused myself and went looking for somewhere to put my beer. I didn't need that bullshit anyway. Volcanoes. Who gives a shit? I mean, really. Who gives a shit?

There wasn't much going on anywhere else either. Everyone in the kitchen was talking about the same shit, about that cult and Brother James. A couple of the girls from Jess' office were drunk as hell and complaining about her and Doc and everything else. They didn't know me from Adam, so I just stood around listening.

Can you believe them? one of the girls said.

I know, another said. She had a martini glass in her and she was sucking it down. They just make me sick, she said.

The first one looked around the corner to make sure neither Jess nor Doc was coming or listening. Between the two of them I could almost scream, she said.

I mean it, the second one said. They make me so gosh dang sick. Sometimes I just want to go up to the both of them while they're talking and just get sick all over them.

I wanted to listen more, but I thought they were probably getting wise to me. I was just standing there, after all. So I went to the fridge and tried to find a place for my beer, but it was filled to the gills and I couldn't even throw one can in there. After a few tries I had to give up. I was going to be carrying that six-pack around with me. That wasn't the worst thing that could happen though. I needed to get lit and I needed to get there in a hurry.

The party was really going at that point, all those people talking about the office and the end of the world and I tried to join in but no one really wanted me around. I didn't make for the best conversation, I guess. I didn't want to talk about that cult or their bullshit signs and anything other than that subject just wasn't going to cut it. And it didn't help that over the talking and music and glasses clinking I could still hear Jess and Doc carrying on and laughing in the other room. It was like they were at another volume from everyone else.

There was this fella, I heard Jess say. This fella who hypnotized himself and—

Gayce, I heard Doc say.

That's right, I heard Jess say and almost scream out of happiness.

Edward Gayce, Doc said.

Yes, Jess said, Yes, yes, yes.

They got louder then, like no one was even around, and just howled together. I looked around the corner and Jess had her hand on the arm of Doc's tux and he was smiling and cleaning out his pipe.

That was all I needed to see. I was tired of all those drunks and the conversations and even Jess and Doc and the only thing I wanted at that point was to watch my game. I needed to find a TV I could switch on and, from the time I'd been there for the cookout, I remembered this second living room toward the end of the house. Doc had given us a full tour when we got there and showed us every last one of his rooms. I remember, Jess had been so impressed that she couldn't stop saying My God, My God every time we saw something new.

I walked through Doc's hallway, away from all the music and chatter, and found that second living room. It was filled with bookcases and books and art and antiques and there was this little area with chairs and couches. The lights were low and I fumbled my way across the floor and grabbed a seat in front of this huge widescreen television.

When I hit power on the remote it came alive and the room lit up. Thing is, I hadn't noticed there were some people already in there. It was this couple all splayed out on one of the couches. They had their clothes on and everything, but they were really going at it. The girl was lying on top of the man and they were moving against each other. They kind of jumped when the television came on. I could see then that the girl was someone I recognized from somewhere. After my eyes adjusted a bit I could see it was Michelle, the girl from work Jess hated so much.

Hey, I said, holding up my beer like I was toasting them, Don't mind me.

Thing is, they got right back to where they were, necking and rubbing each other. I thought that about beat all. What the hell, I thought, and found the Pacers game. I saw they were down in the fourth to Milwaukee and I watched a few plays here and there. But I wasn't paying that close of attention. Not really. Out of the corner of my eye I was watching Michelle and her guy pick up business.

It seemed like they couldn't have given a rat's ass that I was in there. They were too into what they were doing. At least Michelle was. The guy she was with might've been a little put off, but she might've preferred it. At least that's the impression I got from all the moaning and carrying on. And judging by what Jess had told me about her, that shouldn't have surprised me. She said all the time that Michelle was loose and didn't have a drop of shame.

What got me though, what really got me, was how Jess had been like that once. There was a day and age, back when we first hooked up, that she would've got down to business anytime and anywhere.

What about that time in front of George's? I said to her one time, after she brought up Michelle the first time and how she liked to show off. Remember that? I said.

What about it? Jess had said. What does that have to do with anything?

I'd reminded her of the first date we ever went on. It was to this cheap place called George's that served hamburgers and beer and it was rundown, even back then. We'd had a hell of a time, eating and laughing, and by the time we got back to the car we were all over each other. That parking lot was in the middle of town, right on Main Street, and people walking by could see right into the car and see what we were up to. That hadn't stopped Jess though. As soon as she closed her door she'd climbed across the seat and straddled me. And it wasn't like the audience bothered her at all. She went until we couldn't anymore, there.

Jess didn't buy it though.

I still don't see what you're getting at, she said. I don't think that has anything to do with that girl or how slutty she is.

I couldn't explain. I couldn't get my point across, I guess. And I doubt I would've had any more luck if she'd been in there watching that couple. She probably would've taken one look at Michelle grinding on that fella and lost her shit right off.

Looking back, I probably should've excused myself after a while. I mean, I sat there and watched everything there was to watch. That girl, Michelle, even locked eyes with me at one point and gave me a little grin. That should've done it. I should've packed up my beers and found somewhere else to watch Indiana lose. I should've, but I didn't. I sat there and watched them finish up. I sat there and watched them get their clothes together and get dressed.

I had my mind made up right then. I wanted to run back into that party and tell Jess I was ready for a brand new start. I was gonna grab her and tell her I was tired of all the bickering and that we needed to let bygones be. And with that I picked up what was left of my beers and went back to the kitchen and the party. All the people were in the main living room. Some of them were even sitting on the floor. They were watching some movie about the world ending. There were earthquakes and floods and fires and people jumping out of buildings and screaming and killing each other in the streets. There was blood everywhere and bunches of people hiding and crying. Everyone was getting a big kick out of that movie. They were all smiling and laughing. In the middle of the group was Jess, sharing a couch with Doc.

Part of me wanted to march across the room and really have at him. Doc was in pretty good shape, all in all, but I figured if I laid into him without his being ready I could really do some damage. I didn't though. I was too busy looking at how the two of them were sitting. He had his arm around her shoulders and she had her hand on his leg, where anyone could see.

I coughed. It was the only thing I could think of to do. There was a moment of quiet in the movie, I think a plane was going down and everyone was saying their goodbyes, and my cough got Jess' attention. She looked up and her hand moved in a hurry.

Somehow I made my way through the crowd and I grabbed Jess and headed to the closet to get our coats. Doc was off the couch and right behind. People were talking, whispering I guess, and he told everyone to hold on, that he'd be back in a second. The three of us made it outside, where the rain had stopped and there was this smell like wet cardboard in the air.

Honey, Jess said to me, real softly. Honey, she said again.

Let's go, I said. I could feel Doc coming. We'll talk about it in the car.

Doc grabbed my shoulder and wheeled me around. My first thought was to clock him as hard as I could. But I didn't. I turned and there he was, sweat dripping down his red face, that hair of his standing up from the part he'd been wearing.

Hey buddy, he said. I'm sorry. I don't even know what to say.

I told him not to say anything and he nodded and waved sadly to Jess. We got in the car and I turned the key.

Listen, she said. She was scared. Her voice was coming in and out. I. I don't. I looked down and there it was, she said. I didn't mean to, she said.

There it was, I said.

I didn't mean for it, she said. She put that same hand on my knee and pulled it away just as fast. I'm sorry, she said.

I know, I said. I'm sorry, I said.

She started to ask why I was sorry, but stopped. We didn't talk for a while after that. I clicked off the radio and we drove through town. There were still people standing around with signs. Their robes were soaked through and clinging to their bodies. Groups of them had clustered around the billboards that said An End to All Things. They were holding up their signs and singing and dancing and some were setting off bottle rockets that jumped into the sky and popped and sizzled. Jess watched from the car and started to cry.

I let her. There wasn't anything I could say anyway. I let her cry and I pulled into this shopping center on Main Street, a few miles down the road. It was this shopping center where hardly anyone went anymore. There was a dollar store in there, a movie theatre that only had one or two old pictures no one went to see, and a pet store with all the front windows broken out. Sandwiched between them was that restaurant where we'd parked once upon a time, George's. The sign was falling apart and the door had been boarded shut. It'd closed down four or five years earlier and just sat there empty ever since.

I parked out front in the spot closest to the road. It was about as close as I could get to the spot where we'd parked on our first date all those years before. From where we were we could see, a few feet away, another one of those goddamned signs. There were lights shining on it and making those words glow. An End to All Things. A group of four or five were underneath, one of them beating a tambourine and another strumming a guitar. They were still dancing, dancing and singing, but they had noticed our car and were keeping an eye on us. They were watching us is what they were doing.

I shut off the engine and looked at Jess. Her face was wet and all of her make-up had smeared and run. I looked at her and she looked at me. Those people were picking it up at that point, really playing and carrying on as loud as they could, the tempo gathering steam. They were singing 'bout the end, 'bout stars exploding and fires raging, the cup finally running over. Singing 'bout a reckoning as old as time itself. Jess and me sat there, listening. Something was going to happen, by God. Something had to happen.

ABOUT THE AUTHOR

A born and bred Hoosier, Jared Yates Sexton is on the creative writing faculty at Georgia Southern University. *An End to All Things* is his debut story collection.